"You don't believe that I'm in pain?" Massimo said.

Jenny shook her head vigorously. "Not a word."

Massimo grinned and his whole face took on an open softness. He moved his hands on her arms, making small, gentle circles over her shoulders.

"But I am in pain," he said softly. "I am in pain with wanting you, Jenny." He pulled her close against his chest, and she could feel his heart beating.

Thoughts tumbled through Jenny's mind. She had not come to make love again; she had come for an explanation. But here they were, kneeling on the rug, holding each other.

"Oh, Massimo," she whispered, "this isn't what I wanted."

"Then what is it that you want, *cara mia?*" His voice was low in her ear.

Jenny shook her head against his shoulder, nuzzling into the hollow of his neck. She knew what she wanted, to hear him say, "I love you." But that seemed too much to ask . . .

Dear Reader:

June 1983 marked SECOND CHANCE AT LOVE's second birthday—and we have good reason to celebrate! While romantic fiction has continued to grow, SECOND CHANCE AT LOVE has remained in the forefront as an innovative, top-selling romance series. In ever-increasing numbers you, the readers, continue to buy SECOND CHANCE AT LOVE, which you've come to know as the "butterfly books."

During the past two years we've received thousands of letters expressing your enthusiasm for SECOND CHANCE AT LOVE. In particular, many of you have asked: "What happens to the hero and heroine after they get married?"

As we attempted to answer that question, our thoughts led naturally to an exciting new concept—a line of romances based on married love. We're now proud to announce the creation of this new line, coming to you this fall, called TO HAVE AND TO HOLD.

There has never been a series of romances about marriage. As we did with SECOND CHANCE AT LOVE, we're breaking new ground, setting a new precedent. TO HAVE AND TO HOLD romances will be heartwarming, compelling love stories of marriages that remain exciting, adventurous, enriching and, above all, romantic. Each TO HAVE AND TO HOLD romance will bring you two people who love each other deeply. You'll see them struggle with challenges many married couples face. But no matter what happens, their love and commitment will see them through to a brighter future.

We're very enthusiastic about TO HAVE AND TO HOLD, and we hope you will be too. Watch for its arrival this fall. We will, of course, continue to publish six SECOND CHANCE AT LOVE romances every month in addition to our new series. We hope you'll read and enjoy them all!

Warm wishes,

Ellen Edwards

Ellen Edwards
SECOND CHANCE AT LOVE
The Berkley Publishing Group
200 Madison Avenue
New York, N.Y. 10016

GOLDEN ILLUSIONS
SARAH CREWE

**SECOND CHANCE AT LOVE
BOOK**

For John

Chapter 1

THE TAXI SCREECHED to a halt in front of the Milan railroad station, and Jennifer Armstrong peered out the window at the massive building. It looked even busier, larger, and harder to understand than the airport—and that had been hard enough.

The driver waited for his money with an exasperated look on his face. The meter read 11,750 *lire,* and Jenny wondered forlornly if she would ever get used to Italian money, always calculated in the thousands and millions. She fumbled in her purse while the driver tapped his fingers impatiently against the dashboard.

Suddenly the back door of the cab swung open, and a well-dressed businessman, obviously in a hurry, looked in. He noted with an expression of distaste that the cab was still occupied, and then, after only a moment's hesitation, climbed in anyway.

"Signorina," the driver said, *"prego . . ."*

Jenny pushed her heavy red-gold hair back off her face and blew a small puff of air out through pursed lips. She had been on a plane from New York for over seven hours and had spent almost another hour at the airport after she had passed through customs trying to get a taxi.

She had already missed the train to Genoa that her travel agent had carefully selected. And now these two typically self-centered men were behaving as if she were purposely holding them up.

She grabbed a 20,000-*lire* note and pushed it into the driver's hand, waving away his half-hearted attempts to give her change. Retrieving her canvas suitcase and the large, lightweight portfolio in which she kept her design drawings from the floor, she clambered pointedly over the businessman and out of the cab. She smiled at the thought that she had probably rumpled his carefully pressed pants.

Twenty dollars down the drain, she thought to herself as she hurried up the steps to the station. Or at least— calculating a thousand *lire* to the dollar and a reasonable tip—about seven. Simon, had he been here, would have watched the meter rather than the scenery all the way in from the airport and would have had the proper amount counted out even before the taxi stopped. And he probably would have given her a little lecture about when to overtip and when not to.

Jenny shook her head briskly, clearing it of thoughts of Simon. She was on her own now—no Simon to make every decision for her, to undermine her confidence until she could hardly get out of bed in the morning. She thought with a firm smile about the effort it had taken over the last few years to grow away from that, to rebuild herself piece by piece—and finally to file for divorce. Now here she was, in a new country, with a new job . . .

But she *had* missed her train. Jenny stood despairingly in the center of the cavernous station for a moment, then picked out a window that seemed to offer tickets and information and made her way to it.

"Mi dispiace," she said after several moments of trying to explain what she wanted. She tried desperately to recall her brief course in Italian. *"Non capisco."* I *am* sorry, she thought with annoyance, but I really *don't* under-

stand—and the train I want is probably pulling out of the station this very minute.

The ticket agent tried again. His voice was louder, and he pointed with extravagant gestures at the timetable he had smoothed out on the counter between them. Jenny shook her head in frustration. The little knot of people milling around her, waiting to reach the ticket window, was growing annoyed.

Suddenly she felt a hand on her elbow.

"Scusi, signorina," said a deep voice just to her left. Jenny turned her head quickly. The man standing beside her was tall and dark, with wide shoulders accented by the elegant cut of his gray pinstripe suit. Jenny blinked. He was extraordinarily good-looking—as good-looking, she thought momentarily, as Simon.

The man spoke in low, rapid Italian to the ticket clerk, and then, as Jenny's eyes widened in disbelief, he quickly counted out some money and took back a ticket in return. Jenny felt a sudden wave of fury. Would the arrogance of men never end? How dare he simply push ahead and buy a ticket for himself and leave her to fumble on her own?

"Signore!" she said loudly, tired and angry and more than willing to make a scene. But her meager supply of Italian deserted her, and she switched to English. "Just what do you think you're doing? I was here first—"

The man's hand was on her elbow again, and as she spoke he was pulling her away from the window.

"Signorina," he interrupted. His voice was soft and soothing, as if he were speaking to a disturbed child, and he looked at her with wide, steady eyes. "You wanted to go to Genoa, I think." He handed her the ticket he had just purchased.

They were out of the crowd now, and Jenny looked at him more closely. His thick black hair was combed straight back from his broad forehead. His eyes, the color of chestnuts, were deep set and surrounded by black lashes so thick and long they would have been the envy of any New York model. Despite a small smile, his brows seemed perpetually knit together in one continuous slash, like a black flame across his swarthy face. Deep creases lined his cheeks.

He was not at all like Simon, Jenny thought now, surprised. There was something much rougher about his face. He looked as if he would plunge right into the battles that Simon so studiously avoided; pain wouldn't deter him from pursuing—and getting—what he wanted. And yet there was something aloof as well, something remote and even gentle, like the carved faces of Roman generals Jenny had seen in museums. It was a face that held one's attention.

"There is a train for Genoa in ten minutes from track 52," he was saying. "The ticket costs eleven thousand five hundred *lire,* and it is an express train, so there is a surcharge of one thousand five hundred *lire.*"

Jenny set her suitcase and portfolio down, frowning slightly as she tried to translate that into dollars, to decide whether or not that was a reasonable price.

"That's about fifteen dollars all together," the man said. Jenny looked at him sharply.

"I . . . thank you very much," she muttered, her gratitude tinged with irritation at the peremptory way in which this stranger was resolving her problems. "Just a minute, my money's right here—"

"No, please, *signorina.*" He held up his hand, palm forward. Jenny looked up from her purse to find him smiling broadly at her. It was an impressive smile, dazzling white teeth against his coppery-brown skin, and it made his face at once much more open. The deep creases softened into the planes of his high cheeks. Jenny sucked in her breath. He really was astonishingly handsome.

"Consider it a token of Italian–American friendship," he said cheerfully. Then he bowed slightly and turned away, his long strides cutting a swath through the crowded

Milan station like a well-made sailboat slicing through ocean waves.

Jenny watched him go. Her practiced designer's eyes followed the way the European cut of his suit outlined his lithe movements, and she nodded in approval. He might be as arrogant as every other man, but he certainly was a delight to the eye.

She stood a moment longer, catching her breath, and then retrieved her bags and started to turn away. Suddenly the gray suit caught her eye again. The man had stopped abruptly, far enough away now that keeping him located in the crowd was difficult. Jenny squinted.

A woman had brought him to his sudden stop—a small, fair woman with neat blond hair pulled back from the delicate features of her face. She wore a simply cut dress of very light lavender, and even from this distance her skin looked almost translucent. To Jenny, she seemed an island of pale calm in this constantly shifting sea of people. The man embraced her, holding her fragile body close to his muscular one, and then the two figures disappeared down one of the long escalators into the far depths of the great railroad station.

Jenny watched the place where they had been. Of course, that was the sort of woman who would appeal to him—a delicate, fragile woman with every hair in place, undoubtedly subservient to his every whim . . . Jenny was suddenly conscious of her own full figure, of the unruly mass of reddish hair that was constantly out of place, of the perpetual pink in her cheeks, heightened now by all this nervous rushing. With one fierce push at her hair, she turned and went to hunt for track 52.

She dragged her bags onto the sleek gray train marked TRANS-EUROPE EXPRESS with tired relief. It was, she noted with pleasure, what she had always called a "movie train": a long, narrow corridor running the length of each car with half a dozen compartments opening off it. In each compartment, facing seats held four people apiece.

But relief turned to frustration as she passed compartment after compartment jammed full of people, their elbows all held tightly against their bodies so as not to jostle one another. There were no vacant seats, and Jenny didn't relish the thought of standing for a two- or three-hour journey.

The fourth car was different. The compartments were upholstered in plush blue and gray, and the sliding doors leading into them were a distinctive smoked glass. Even the corridor was carpeted. *And* there were empty seats. There was a reason, Jenny suspected, why all those jammed-together people hadn't come here to find seats, but she was too tired to bother figuring it out.

She shifted her portfolio into her left hand and began struggling with one of the sliding doors. Almost instantly a conductor appeared, his hands upraised.

"Signorina, scusi, è primo, primo classo." He stood in front of her, smiling politely but effectively blocking her way into the compartment. He gestured to the cars through which she had just come.

"Secondo," he said firmly.

So that was it. This was a first-class coach, for which she would have to pay more, and her ticket was for second class.

Jenny put on her most winning smile. "I have a ticket," she said cheerfully, waving the little piece of cardboard in front of him as if that solved everything. Then she changed her expression to woebegone. "And there aren't any seats back there."

The conductor shook his head and made a little clucking sound. *"Mi dispiace, signorina. È primo. Anche riservato."* He tapped a forefinger against the little sign taped to the door of the compartment, on which were listed several names. *"Tutto riservato."*

Jenny sighed in resignation and reached for her purse. Her ticket, after all, had been a gift; she was quite willing to pay a little something for a comfortable seat. And there were clearly seats here.

She glanced into the compartment again. Only three men in it. There was lots of room. She started to open her purse when something made her swing her head back toward the compartment. One of the men wore a gray pinstripe suit. His face had been hidden by a newspaper. But now he was folding the newspaper and rising from his seat by the window.

Jenny groaned. Not again. But there was nothing to be done, no opening in the floor of the corridor into which she could sink out of sight. The man had already taken the necessary two strides to bring himself out into the corridor, and now he stepped between Jenny and the conductor, his back to her.

"Excuse me," Jenny said through clenched teeth. "I can handle this myself."

But the man had already done whatever was needed, and a moment later the conductor was on his way, whistling softly to himself and knocking on the door of the next compartment.

The tall man turned to face Jenny, tucking his leather wallet back into an inside jacket pocket. With a small bow and an ironic smile, he held the compartment door open for her and gestured her in.

"Your mouth is open," he said. Jenny snapped it shut.

"Thank you ... once again," she said, a tight smile on her face. "But I really could have managed for myself."

"Oh, I'm quite sure you could," the man replied. He swung her suitcase and portfolio onto the wide overhead rack and pointed to the window seat that he had been occupying himself.

"I don't normally make a habit of being rescued," Jenny said, still standing in the space between the facing seats.

The man had sat down near the door and picked up his newspaper again. He looked at her from heavy-lidded eyes. "I'm quite sure you don't," he said.

Jenny pulled her purse open. "In any case, I can pay you what I owe you now. For the ticket. Eleven thousand, you said, plus whatever you paid just now . . . ?"

The man's eyebrows rose, and his smile widened slightly. "Eleven thousand five hundred," he said. "Plus one thousand five hundred supplement for the express. Plus another six thousand for the first class reservation."

Jenny blinked and pressed her lips together. Her supply of Italian money was dwindling fast; she would have to cash another traveler's check as soon as she arrived in Genoa.

There was a loud whistle, and Jenny's purse jumped in her hand as the train suddenly lurched forward. She reached to salvage its contents, but lipstick, compact, and a jumble of Italian bills and change spilled out.

"Please, do sit down," the man said. Jenny sat, leaning over to gather up her things. He handed her the lipstick and some change. Then Jenny grimly counted out the money—19,000 *lire*. She handed the notes to the man, who accepted them with a silent nod and tucked them carefully into his wallet.

"Grazie mille, signorina," he said when the wallet was back in his pocket. There was a note of amusement in his voice. "A thousand thanks."

The two other passengers in the compartment, both older, distinguished-looking businessmen, were engrossed in paperwork that they had laid out on the seat between them. The dark man sat on Jenny's side of the compartment, near the door, with his body turned slightly toward her. His long legs were stretched out between the facing seats so that his feet almost touched her own. His shoes were obviously expensive leather and highly polished. Probably handmade, Jenny thought absently. His hands were in his pockets, and the newspaper lay abandoned on the seat.

"This was my fault, of course—this second rescue,"

the man said as Jenny finally settled herself more or less comfortably against the plush seat. "I bought you a second-class ticket, and I should have known better." His eyes swept casually over her body. "You are, of course, a first-class type."

Jenny looked steadily past him at the smoked glass door. She was suddenly conscious of her Halston jacket and pants—her only designer outfit—and felt irrationally grateful that she had chosen to wear them rather than the jeans and turtleneck she had originally considered. Suddenly a picture of the blond woman in her pale dress flitted into her head.

"Second class was full," she said stiffly.

"Ah." The man nodded. "I thought perhaps you had come especially to find me."

"Second class was full," she repeated stubbornly, pushing at her hair as it once more slid over one eye. "I was looking for a place to sit. I had no idea you'd even gotten on this train."

"Ah." He shrugged. "I thought perhaps your conscience—or your independence—had gotten the better of you, and you wished to find me to repay your debt."

Jenny turned her head toward the window and fixed her eyes on the last pillar of the station platform as it receded into the distance. How stupid. Of course, that was what he had meant in the first place—that she might be looking for him to pay him back. It was remarkable, really, how she still saw Simon's self-centered flirtatiousness in every man.

She turned back from the window and let a soft smile settle on her full lips.

"I'm sorry if I've caused you any trouble," she said. "I'm glad I've had the chance to pay you back. I . . . I don't like to be obligated to people."

He nodded, and his deep brown eyes sparkled with amusement. "Especially to men, perhaps."

Jenny looked at him steadily. "Perhaps," she replied.

"So, *signorina,* you are going to Genoa."

Jenny felt her body relax slightly, as though they had come to the very edge of a dangerous ravine and then stepped back. She nodded.

"Yes, I have a job there. For six months. Sort of an apprenticeship."

The man's thick eyebrows rose.

"A job? Now that is interesting. Genoa is not a city to which many Americans come. What will you be doing there?"

Jenny felt the excitement about her new position sweep over her. She leaned forward on her seat.

"I'm a designer—a fashion designer. I'll be working with Gabriella Fortuna for six months. I'm terribly lucky: I applied ages ago, with lots of other people, but she just sent the acceptance a few weeks ago. It's all very exciting—she's a wonderful designer with a very big, international reputation..." Jenny stopped talking, experiencing a sudden twinge of embarrassment at her own flood of enthusiasm.

The man leaned his head back against the upholstery and nodded slowly. His smile had disappeared, and there was something masklike and remote about his face.

"That does sound exciting," he agreed. He studied Jenny gravely from beneath his long black lashes.

Jenny looked back at him, feeling her cheeks turn pinker than usual from enthusiasm and embarrassment. She was uncomfortably conscious of her fresh, very American face: the wide-set brown eyes and slightly too-full mouth, the dusting of freckles across her nose. Whatever makeup she had put on before boarding the plane last night had long since worn off, and she hadn't bothered to renew it. There were, she suspected, the beginnings of dark circles under her eyes, and her hair, she was quite sure, was its usual tumbled mess.

Once again the pale, fine-featured face of the woman

in Milan came vividly to mind, and Jenny shifted uncomfortably in her seat.

"You will like Genoa," the man finally said. "It's a very special place. A big city—the largest port in Europe—but with a sense of history and leisure. Not like Milano—not pushing and shoving all the time."

The two businessmen looked up from their paper with sour expressions, and the man nodded politely to them. Jenny smiled.

"Milan *was* a little overwhelming," she confessed. She hesitated for a moment. "Are you . . . are you from Genoa?" she asked tentatively. All at once it seemed terribly important to know if this man, whose dark good looks so reminiscent of Simon's both attracted and frightened her, was going to the same place she was.

"*Si*, I am *Genovese*," he answered, and the businessmen exchanged knowing glances. "Perhaps, since we are going to the same place, we should introduce ourselves. I am Massimo Silvano. My family is in banking in Genoa."

The businessmen both glanced up, expressions of interest on their faces.

"I'm Jennifer Armstrong," Jenny responded. "Jenny."

She held out her hand a little awkwardly, and Massimo Silvano raised it quickly to his lips. She could feel the warmth and hardness of his mouth against the back of her hand.

Then his eyes fell to her left hand, still in her lap. "*Signorina* Armstrong," he said. "It *is signorina*, is it not?"

Jenny pulled back the hand he held and folded it over her ringless left one.

"Do you mean, am I married or not?" she asked.

He nodded.

"Yes," she said firmly. "I mean no, I'm not married—yes, it is *signorina*."

"I see," he said, nodding again. "You have never been married?"

"I really don't . . ." Jenny looked down at her hands. There's really no point, she thought to herself, in playing games of evasion. "I have been married, but I'm not now," she finally said softly.

"And that is why you don't want to be obligated to men. Because you were married to a man who demanded too much from you."

He said it as though he knew it was true, and Jenny once again had the uncanny feeling that he could read her mind. One of the businessmen had stopped reading and looked over the top of his half-glasses with a small smile, evidently enjoying the way the conversation was going. Jenny looked sharply at Massimo.

"And now," he went on, "you are ready to make your own demands, rather than let others make demands of you. To take lovers, perhaps, but on your own terms."

Jenny stared at him. Her mouth fell open, and she snapped it shut. The man in the opposite seat had put down his papers and dropped all pretense of working. He looked back and forth from Massimo to Jenny as if following a tennis match.

Massimo's eyes were bright with amusement. He held one hand up, palm forward, as he had back at the Milan station.

"Don't worry," he said. "I am not applying for the job. I admire women who know their own minds and who do things for themselves, but I like to be permitted to do things for them sometimes myself, without feeling I have insulted them."

Jenny stared at him for a moment longer. He was, after all, just like Simon, she thought—just like all men: self-centered, so sure of himself. She pushed fiercely at a lock of hair that had fallen over her forehead and then turned away from him, reaching for her purse where it sat on the floor.

"If you'll excuse me," she said icily, "I should look over some papers."

The men opposite frowned slightly and returned to their own work.

Jenny pulled her purse open and fumbled through it, hunting for something that looked vaguely businesslike. Finally she pulled out a letter that had arrived just as she was locking up her apartment, the last letter she had received from Gabriella Fortuna. As with all of Gabriella's letters, the writing was spidery and European in lavender ink on pale green paper. Jenny had barely skimmed through it on the way to the airport.

Now she read through the letter two or three times, making her eyes stop at each word, although her mind refused to focus on anything except the sharp, fascinating profile of the man sitting next to her. Then a word in the text caught her eye—a name. She looked at it again, then glanced quickly at Massimo Silvano. He had picked up his newspaper and was reading it, his eyes wandering lazily over the pages.

"*Scusi,*" Jenny said hesitantly.

He lowered his paper slightly and looked at her.

"Do you happen to know a *Luca* Silvano in Genoa?"

Massimo folded his paper carefully and put it back on the seat.

"I have a brother named Luca," he said.

Jenny blew a quick puff of air out between her lips.

"I had forgotten the name," she said hurriedly. "I...Everything was such a rush just before I left."

He was looking at her curiously now, his eyes wider than she had yet seen them. There was, she noticed abstractedly, a tiny rim of gold around the dark brown centers; it was hardly noticeable beneath the usually hooded lids, but when he opened his eyes wide, the gold gleamed and sparkled.

"This is a letter from *Madama* Fortuna," she explained. "She has been saying all along that she would find me an apartment to live in, but apparently that turned out to be very difficult...Anyway, here's what she says..." Jenny followed the passage in the letter with her finger as she read. "'Alas, I find you no apartment. On the Riviera, in the summer, this comes to be impossible.'" Jenny looked up with a smile. "Her English is a little unusual," she said.

"Anyway, she goes on, 'But my good friend, name is Luca Silvano, graciously offers the space of a room in his family's apartment. The Silvanos are my oldest and dearest friends, and this will be fine. Address is...' and then she gives the address."

Jenny looked at Massimo expectantly. He had raised his eyes to the ceiling of the compartment. There was a smile on his lips, but he was shaking his head slowly.

"So," he said, still not looking at her. "So you will be staying with me in Genoa, *Signorina* Armstrong."

The businessmen both put down their papers and stared openly at Massimo.

"With you!" Jenny cried. In the very pit of her stomach she felt something turn over slowly, as though some living thing, long asleep, were waking up and stretching. She swallowed hard.

"That's impossible," she said firmly. "I couldn't possibly stay with you. I'll find a hotel."

Massimo raised his hands to his face and rubbed his eyes with the backs of his knuckles, like a little boy awakening from a nap. Then he turned to look at Jenny, a smile fixed on his lips but his eyes flat and impenetrable.

"Of course it is possible, *Signorina* Armstrong. *Madama* Fortuna has arranged it, and whatever *Madama* Fortuna arranges..." He paused for a moment, and his smile grew into an affectionate grin. Jenny caught a fleeting glimpse of the gold in his eyes. "Whatever *Madama* Fortuna arranges," he repeated, "occurs."

"But you obviously knew nothing about this. You

didn't even mention that you *knew Madama* Fortuna when I said I was going to work for her . . . and besides, it's . . . it's not . . ."

"*Signorina,* I have been in Milano for two weeks. My brother Luca has made the offer, and he has simply neglected to tell me about it. My brother Luca often forgets to tell me such things. I am sure that all the preparations have been made, and that my family expects you."

Jenny blinked. Family. It had never occurred to her, not once, that Massimo Silvano might be married.

Now she protested again weakly. "But your wife—" she began.

"My wife is dead," he snapped, interrupting. Then he went on more gently. "She died three years ago. Soon after the birth of our second child." His voice was steady and emotionless.

"I'm so sorry," Jenny murmured. "I had no idea . . ."

"Of course not. It was an auto accident. She was on her way to meet a lover."

The businessmen across the aisle suddenly made a show of being engrossed in their own affairs once again, and Massimo glanced at them, amused.

Jenny fiddled with the small jade ring on the middle finger of her right hand. *My wife is dead.* The words echoed in her ears. Whatever had been stirring deep inside her shifted again, touching the very roots of her sexual being. He had been unhappily married, and now he was free . . .

"Then your family is you and your brother . . . ?" she asked.

"And my children. No, *signorina,* the apartment of men alone would be unsuitable for a young lady. Even our dear, unconventional, sometimes muddled Gabriella would recognize that." Again, Jenny detected a note of real affection in Massimo's voice when he spoke of her new employer, and she wondered what their relationship was. "There are my two children and our housekeeper. Luca does not really live with us—he is in and out. We keep a room for him when he needs it. And you will have the guest room."

Jenny nodded slowly. It was all too fast—too fast and too confusing. This man had been a stranger an hour ago, and an irritating stranger at that, and now she was to live in his house, see him every day...Part of her said to run as fast as she could in the opposite direction, but part of her felt a joyous reawakening, a renewal of life that she hadn't felt in eight long years.

"You have children?" Massimo asked.

Jenny shook her head. "No, no children."

"But you wanted children," he said softly. It was a statement, not a question, and again Jenny had the uncanny feeling that he could see what she was thinking.

"Yes," she agreed. "But my husband..."

Massimo looked away. "I see."

Suddenly the tiredness of the last twenty-four hours swept over Jenny like an ocean wave. Every limb, every muscle felt limp with exhaustion. It wasn't just the hours of travel; it was the accumulated tension of the past five weeks—even of the past eight years.

It was, a year ago, finally gathering the courage to walk out on the man she had once thought she loved, the man who insisted on making every decision for her, on choosing her jewelry and her friends and her job. It was a year of living alone in a tiny apartment, paying most of her earnings to a lawyer, giving Simon everything he wanted just to be free. It was the moment five weeks ago when the final divorce papers had arrived, and Simon had called, almost in tears, begging her to come back—and she had felt, not relieved, but merely tired.

And then it was the new job, the incredibly rash decision she had made to give up New York and cut all the ties, to prove once and for all that she could do things on her own...to come to Genoa where she knew no one, and no one knew her. No one except this uncanny, brash man, a stranger who in an instant seemed to know her so well.

Jenny rested her head back against the seat. Exhaustion overtook her. She was no longer aware of the man next to her, or even of the low green mountains that ranged beside the train, the blur of scenery. Jenny closed her eyes, giving in to sleep...

The sailboat moved easily, gliding across the soft blue surface of the Mediterranean. With her in the open cabin was a tall, dark-haired man, his coppery skin gleaming with sweat and salt water in the brilliant heat of the Riviera sun. He wore white swim trunks, and his muscles formed distinct rippling patterns beneath the smooth skin of his upper arms and his thighs as he moved about the boat. He came to stand beside her. His face was handsome—Simon's face. But no, the features were too sharp, the creases too deep, almost like knife scars. It wasn't Simon's face; it was too harsh and yet too gentle.

He draped one arm casually about Jenny's shoulders, and she could feel the tickling warmth as the dark hairs of his forearm brushed against her own hot, dry skin. She slid her arm around his waist, feeling the hard strength of his muscles beneath the palm of her hand.

But suddenly the sea grew choppy. The progress of the boat seemed to stop, and the waves seemed to shake her body, as if some force were pulling at her...

Jenny's eyes flew open. Massimo Silvano was leaning across her, his face very close to her own. His right hand held her left arm, and he was shaking it vigorously. Her own right arm lay behind him on the seat, resting against the warm, fine wool of his jacket. The train was still, and the compartment was now empty and dim.

"*Signorina*...Jenny," he said softly. "We are in Genoa. *Signorina!*" He gave her arm another shake.

Jenny stared at him blankly for a moment.

"*Buon giorno,* Jenny," he said with an amused nod. "You have been sleeping."

His face was only inches from hers, and Jenny could see the soft gleam of gold in his eyes even though his heavy lids were almost closed.

"I'm awake," she said, her voice almost a whisper.

He didn't move. She could feel the warmth of his hand on her arm, and his breath was soft and warm against her face. Her own eyes were still half-closed, and her mouth was slightly parted as it had been in sleep. Nervously, she ran her tongue quickly over her full lower lip.

Massimo Silvano closed his eyes for the briefest of moments, and Jenny was suddenly acutely aware that only some force of will was preventing him from moving even closer, from discovering for himself what her lips tasted like. And Jenny wondered urgently how his own hard mouth would feel against hers, how her softness and his hardness would meld into one.

Her eyes widened and she shifted in her seat, pulling her arm from behind him as though it belonged to a stranger. He stood up, and his eyes were hooded now, his face masklike.

"I'm afraid we must get off quickly, *signorina,* or we shall find ourselves in Roma with the train. I don't think that is your intention, and I know it is not mine."

Jenny sat up, briskly smoothing her rust-colored slacks, the sleeves of her beige jacket, and her untidy hair.

"I'm sorry," she said, getting to her feet. "I didn't realize I'd fallen asleep."

Massimo swung her suitcase and portfolio down from the overhead rack, and Jenny could see the muscles in his wide back working beneath the fabric of his suit. She remembered the man in her dream, the patterns of his muscles, the feel of his hard back against the palm of her hand.

Massimo had only a slim leather briefcase, and Jenny

wondered if she had misunderstood when he said he had been away two weeks. He handed her the portfolio and took her suitcase and his briefcase in one hand, then slid the other under her elbow and led her quickly off the train. The conductor waved and winked as they stepped down onto the concrete platform, and Jenny saw across from them a large sign in peeling white paint: GENOVA.

She shrugged her shoulder bag more securely into place and blew a tiny, triumphant blast of air upward toward her unruly hair. Even through the fumes of the railroad station she could smell the moist air of the Mediterranean. She felt a sudden, sweet burst of freedom, and she took a quick little skip down the platform. No one would run her life here. She was free, and she would do just as she wished—and she would trust to her own good judgment, so carefully nurtured in this last year, that her wishes wouldn't lead to disaster.

But even as she thought all that, Jenny glanced at Massimo Silvano, walking beside her toward the terminal and smiling with amusement at her skips and grins. Everything about him signaled danger. *He* was disaster— disaster in the person of yet another man, charming and beautiful and arrogant, who could take over her life. Whatever had begun to stir in her depths stretched once again. And at that moment Jenny realized with something akin to terror that if Massimo Silvano decided he wanted her, there would be very little she could do except give in.

Chapter 2

JENNY WAS MENTALLY reviewing her history. The original city of Genoa had been built on a narrow plain between a natural, semicircular harbor and a low range of coastal mountains. The medieval Genovese had strung forts along the mountain crests and then sat back, smugly secure from attack by their rivals, Venice and Parma. Later, as hostilities among cities grew less frequent and the population grew larger, the city expanded helter-skelter up the mountainsides, and finally it spilled over the tops and down the far slopes. Now Massimo Silvano steered his silver-gray Fiat through the narrow streets climbing the hillside.

Finally he pulled the car to a stop at a building that nestled against the side of the hill, its top story opening onto the very crest of a promontory that overlooked the harbor. Gathering up their bags, he accompanied Jenny to the building's thick oak doors, which opened into a small foyer containing an old-fashioned, open metalwork elevator.

As Jenny and Massimo entered the foyer, a door opposite them flew open and two small figures bounded out.

"Papà! Papà!" they cried in unison, one grasping Massimo's knees and the other pulling at both hands. He set down the bags and lifted the children in his arms.

"Ciao, Nino. *Come va,* Angelina *cara?* Mmmm..." He buried his face against theirs, planting big kisses on their cheeks. Jenny stood awkwardly watching, and she felt the barest touch of tears in her eyes. If only I had chosen a husband wisely, she told herself.

Then Massimo turned to her, still cradling the children in his arms. His face was split by a dazzling grin, and his features hid nothing: all was love.

"Signorina Armstrong," he said, "these are my children." He set them down and they stood at his sides, each holding a hand. He nodded at the little boy, who appeared to be seven or eight, with dark hair and huge, solemn eyes. "This is Nino. And this is my daughter Angela." Jenny looked at the exquisitely round little girl, her head a tangle of golden-red curls. Both children stared at her gravely.

"Buon giorno," she said with a smile. *"Sono...* *sono..."* She looked at Massimo for help.

"Don't worry," he laughed. "They both speak English. Or at least Nino speaks English. Angelina shouts it."

Jenny smiled. "Hello. I'm delighted to meet you both."

The children continued to stare for a moment, and then Nino bowed formally in response. The little girl tugged at her father's hand until he leaned toward her, and she whispered something in his ear. Massimo nodded and let go of her hand. She came to Jenny in one bounce, curtsied gaily, then grasped her hand tightly and pulled her across the foyer.

"Come, *signorina,* you must see your room!"

Jenny let herself be tugged along, looking over her shoulder at Massimo, who shrugged and waved her on, grinning.

"Go on," he said. "Nino and I will bring your things in a moment."

Angela led Jenny on into the apartment, through a small entrance hall and into a long corridor. Jenny caught a fleeting glimpse of a large, elegantly furnished living room off to the right with a grand piano in one corner and, at the far end, a set of glass doors, apparently leading to a terrace.

"We have been so excited!" Angela was saying. "Ever since *zio* Luca told us you would be coming. A lady from America! *Papà* often has guests from America, but they are men always, in business . . ." Angela turned her head so that Jenny could see her exaggerated frown. "No fun." Her grin returned. "You will be fun," she declared.

Angela threw open a door halfway down the long corridor. Jenny sucked in her breath and then blew a little bit out. The room was large and luxurious, furnished with exquisite taste and, Jenny was sure, not a little money. Richly shaded Persian carpets covered most of the floor, and what remained exposed was beautiful polished wood. A variety of small prints and drawings hung on the cream-colored walls. The furniture was obviously old and valuable: a big, carved double bed with a satiny quilt, a softly gleaming wooden trunk, an ornately carved wardrobe as big as three closets set side by side, a deep, chintz-covered armchair, several brass lamps, and, beside the door, a modern, butcher-block worktable with its own attached gooseneck lamp. That had obviously been put here for her benefit, and Jenny wondered who had thought of it.

Angela scurried about, switching on lamps, throwing open the doors of the wardrobe to show Jenny the full-length mirror and variety of drawers and shelves, and bouncing on the bed to prove its softness. Jenny looked around with a satisfied smile.

There was a knock on the door, and Angela pulled it

open. Massimo came in and dropped Jenny's suitcase on the bed while Nino struggled manfully with the portfolio.

"Everything is suitable?" Massimo asked politely. He was smiling, but his face had lost the joyous spontaneity it had held when he had greeted his children.

Jenny nodded enthusiastically. "It's delightful," she proclaimed. "Just perfect."

Massimo looked quickly around the room, raising his eyebrows slightly when he caught sight of the worktable. Turning back to Jenny, he announced, "You will need some time. Dinner is at eight-thirty." He glanced at his watch. "It is almost six now. Please make yourself comfortable and then come and have a drink. Nino, Angela, *dài!* Come, come." He turned toward the door, Nino at his heels, but Angela remained on the bed.

"Angelina!" he said more firmly. "The *signorina* has things to do, and it's almost suppertime for you. *Dài!*"

"Oh, please, *Papà!*" the little girl moaned.

"It's all right, really," Jenny interceded on her behalf. "Angela can help me unpack."

Angela looked beseechingly at her father. Massimo hesitated a moment and then shrugged, turned away, and closed the door behind him.

Jenny unpacked the canvas suitcase quickly and efficiently, shaking out dresses and skirts and handing them to Angela to hang in the wardrobe. They stacked underwear and sweaters in its deep drawers, and slipped jeans and nightgowns over the hooks at its back.

Jenny had decided almost as soon as Gabriella Fortuna's offer had come to carry only those clothes that she could fit into one suitcase and to fill in after she arrived. Now she was glad; she had selected carefully and had brought only those things she really loved.

Angela looked critically through Jenny's small collections of jewelry and makeup, laying them out carefully on the shelf opposite the mirror.

"You have few things," the little girl said thoughtfully, "but very nice."

Jenny nodded, amused. "Thank you, Angela. I did leave some things at home."

Angela nodded solemnly. "What's in here?" she asked, indicating the large portfolio.

"That's part of my work—my drawings," Jenny answered, unzipping the case. She pulled out one of several large sketch pads and some pencils. "See?" she said, opening the pad to a sketch of some slacks and a jacket.

"Ah, *si*," Angela replied. "*Zio* Luca told us—you will work for *zia* Gabriella, no?"

Jenny nodded. "That's right. *Zia*," she repeated. "Does that mean aunt?"

"*Si,* but Gabriella is not our real aunt. Just our pretend aunt. Can I draw something?"

Jenny settled Angela at the worktable with paper and pencils while she showered in the blue-tiled bathroom. She noted with pleasure the heated towel racks. Simon would be green with envy if he could see all this, she thought idly. She let the hot water cascade over her breasts and belly, feeling the grime of her hours of travel rinse away. She wanted more than anything to wash her hair, but a hair dryer was one of the things she had planned to buy here, to make sure it would work on Italian current. Instead, she gave her unruly tresses a vigorous brushing.

Back in the bedroom Jenny pulled on fresh underwear and a simple wraparound dress of soft, lightweight wool. Angela watched as Jenny applied a quick brush of pink to her cheeks, and another of blue across her eyelids.

"You are so pretty," the little girl said with a frown. "How can you be so pretty when you wear such little makeup? My *zia* Miriam wears all the makeup, and she is still not so pretty."

Jenny laughed. "That's very sweet of you to say, Angela. Thank you." She studied her face in the mirror a moment longer, then picked up two tortoiseshell combs from the small pile of jewelry, pushing them into her shining hair just behind her ears in a despairing attempt to control it.

"Who is *zia* Miriam?" she asked casually. "Another pretend aunt?"

The little girl shrugged. "She lives in Milano," she said. "She come to visit sometime."

Jenny felt a tiny stab of cold. "You have a lot of aunts," she said, trying to keep her voice light.

Angela shrugged again. Then her face lit up with a grin. "*Zia* Gabriella wear all the makeup, too," she said mischievously. "So much sometime you cannot see her face! But *zia* Gabriella, she is so funny." Angela climbed onto the big bed and bounced several times. "I love *zia* Gabriella."

Jenny turned away from the mirror with a smile. "Good," she said. "I hope I will, too."

"Oh, *everybody* love *zia* Gabriella. Especially Papa."

Jenny looked at the little girl a moment longer, wondering. Then she asked, "Well, do I look okay?"

"*Si*, very pretty, *signorina!* Now can we go see what Rosa cooks for supper?"

"Of course," Jenny affirmed with a nod.

Angela led her back down the long corridor and through the entrance hall. Then the little girl pushed open a door, and they were in a huge, warm kitchen—a room almost as big as the entire New York apartment where Jenny had lived the past year. It was tiled in white and blue, with big white cabinets and appliances, and scurrying around in it was a small, round woman in her sixties with a snowy white apron tied around her ample waist.

"Rosa!" Angela called. The woman turned her head.

"Ah!" she cried. "*La signorina Americana! Signorina, buona sera, ben'venuto à Italia! Come va, signorina—stanca?*"

Jenny looked at her, bewildered, and Angela laughed delightedly. "Rosa speaks no English," she explained. "She is asking you if you are tired."

"Ah, *si*." Jenny nodded. "*Si, stanca. Sono stanca.*"

"Ah, *si*," Rosa repeated, "*stanca*." She made quick tapping gestures with her hands. All her motions were quick, reminding Jenny of the first robins of spring, with their puffed-up breasts and their tiny, jerky movements.

"*Prego, signorina, sedéte!*" Rosa waved at the large table in the middle of the room, and for the first time Jenny noticed that solemn little Nino was already sitting there, a large bowl of soup in front of him. He smiled shyly at her.

"She says to sit down," he said softly.

Jenny stayed with the children as they tore through their suppers, and when Rosa noticed the time, Jenny offered to put them both to bed. It was nearly eight o'clock when she emerged from Nino's room, feeling relaxed and content. There was something about a child's bedtime ritual that left one so satisfied.

Massimo had said to come have a drink, but she had no idea where to find him. Hesitantly, Jenny turned into the living room, but it was silent and empty. She glanced around the room, taking in the rich carpets, the lovely antique furniture, and the obviously good paintings on the wall. On top of the grand piano was a collection of photographs in gleaming silver frames, and Jenny paused to study them.

There were, predictably, a number of the children: alone, together, with their father, with another dark, handsome man whom Jenny assumed was their Uncle Luca. One showed Angela as a baby and Nino at about three with a classically beautiful woman—their mother, presumably. Jenny studied the photo a moment, searching the woman's face for a hint of what she had been like. But there were no clues—only a cool formality.

A little exclamation escaped Jenny as she caught sight of another picture, and she smiled as she recognized the image. Gabriella Fortuna's long, almost skinny, body and her large, angular features—saved from homeliness

by her striking vibrance and intelligence—were unmistakable. Jenny's new boss stared straight at the camera
with a great grin, the makeup Angela had mentioned
adding an air of eccentric exoticism.

A second photo showed Gabriella with the children
on a beach, her long legs covered by an extraordinary
purple and yellow skirt. In the third shot she stood next
to Massimo Silvano, smiling at him with the same intensity she had shown for the camera in the first picture.
She was, Jenny noticed, almost Massimo's height. Once
again she wondered just what sort of relationship Gabriella Fortuna and Massimo Silvano had.

Jenny started to turn away from the photos when one
more, tucked to the back, stopped her. It was a snapshot
of a very fair woman wearing a pale pink dress. The
breeze had caught her dress so that it outlined her small,
high breasts and tiny waist, her elegantly shaped legs.
But her blond hair was precisely in place, pulled carefully
back from her face. She was smiling slightly, looking
just to one side of the camera. At the bottom of the
picture was an inscription: *"Con passione grande, tua
Miriam."*

"With great love, your Miriam." Jenny looked at the
words a moment longer, transfixed. Then she moved her
glance to the face. In the woman's eyes was an expression
of total devotion, of abject adoration. It was a private
and disturbing expression, almost painful to see, and
Jenny quickly looked away. She didn't want to think
about the relationship between this woman and the photographer—for the woman was the same one she had
seen at the Milan station. And the photographer, Jenny
had no doubt, was Massimo Silvano.

She turned abruptly, escaping the snapshot, and looked
around the room. The double glass doors stood open to
what Jenny had guessed was a terrace, and she stepped
out into the cool night air.

The terrace was huge. It ran the length of the building

and was perhaps twenty feet wide, enclosed by a low stone wall topped with a waist-high wrought iron railing. Set at intervals were tubs of geraniums, just beginning to show their scarlet in the early warmth of the Italian spring. It was dark now, and the terrace was only dimly lit by several small lamps affixed to the back wall.

Jenny walked to the edge of the terrace and looked out over the city of Genoa. Lights glimmered all the way down the hillside, and at the bottom glittering neon signs—not the jangling, straightforward colors of New York, but rather soft oranges and enchanting pastels—formed an ever-changing pattern of color among the downtown buildings. Great *piazze* shone with light, and car headlights formed ribbons of yellow and white along the winding streets.

Closer to the harbor was a crescent of darkness, a small half-moon of fewer lights, and, it seemed to Jenny, smaller, more crowded buildings. Beyond, on the black water, gray tankers and looming black cargo ships, outlined by the yellow lamps of the piers, shared space with glistening white cruise liners, lit up as if for extravagant parties. All the ships shone brightly against the vast, black velvet sea.

Jenny stood silently, her hands on the iron railing, her eyes entranced by this first vision of her new city at night.

"So, *signorina*, you find it impressive?"

Jenny turned, startled. Only then did she see Massimo Silvano, his tall body silhouetted by the lamps, just a few yards behind her.

"*Signore* Silvano," she said, nodding her head in his direction.

"Please," he said, holding up his hand. "Massimo."

Jenny ducked her head. "Massimo," she repeated. Then she looked up at him again. "I'm sorry, I didn't know you were here." His face was in shadow, but Jenny was aware of its sharp, carved lines and the deep gleam of his hooded eyes. He looked, she thought again with irritation, very much like Simon.

He bowed slightly and moved toward her, smiling. He held a glass in one hand. "Would you like a drink?"

Jenny nodded. "Thank you. Some wine would be very nice."

She watched as he moved back to a small cart that stood by a second set of glass doors and poured white wine into a cut glass goblet. As she had been at the Milan station, Jenny found herself impressed by the grace and sureness of his movements—a self-confidence that Simon, despite his arrogance, had never had. Massimo returned and handed her the glass.

"You are enjoying the view?" he asked again.

Jenny smiled. "You'd think I'd be immune to night skylines after eight years in New York. But there's something..." She looked out again over the softly glowing city. "Something softer and warmer about this... more human. In New York, the lights seem to go on forever; there's wonder, but no mystery. Here there's that great blackness out there, the sea..."

Massimo smiled. He stood beside her now, looking out toward the port. "Tourists rarely come to Genoa," he said. He paused for a moment and laughed lightly. "For which I am very grateful. Perhaps because it is such a commercial city, such a busy port, and it has no single great attraction, as Milan has its cathedral and 'The Last Supper.' But to me, Genoa is particularly beautiful."

His hand brushed Jenny's arm as he gestured at the darker crescent of jumbled buildings at the edge of the harbor.

"That is *centro storico*, the historical center of the city, around which the original walls stood. You can still see bits and pieces of the walls, with their four gates. Those buildings have been there since the Middle Ages, and they are still in use, still alive. *Centro* is the heart of Genoa."

He shrugged, and Jenny could feel the movement of his arm against her own. "Genoa has a *reality*," he went on, "that the tourist cities like Venice and Florence, for all their beauty, lack. It does not have their wistfulness, but then . . ." He turned toward Jenny. "I am not fond of wistfulness. I prefer life."

Jenny looked at him and blinked, almost instinctively taking a step backward. Her foot brushed against the low stone wall and she stumbled slightly, steadying herself against the iron railing. Massimo set his glass down on the flat top of the stone wall and reached toward her with both hands, letting one settle on her shoulder and, with the other, straightening the tortoiseshell combs. Jenny could feel the heavy warmth of his hand on her arm, but his fingertips seemed almost weightless against the thickness of her hair. She stood motionless as his strong fingers brushed a loose strand from her forehead.

"You are full of life, Jenny," he whispered. He let his other hand fall to her shoulder as well, and he began moving his fingers slowly, making tiny circles over her neck, her arms, her upper back. Jenny felt her breath come more quickly, and a tiny pulse at the side of her neck began hammering. She wondered that the noise of it didn't make him step away.

His hands slid down to her waist and pressed at the small of her back, urging her closer until she stood almost against him, the tips of her breasts just grazing his chest, her hips barely touching the angular hardness of his own. Her eyes widened momentarily and then fluttered shut as his mouth descended onto hers. The moment on the train, when she had wondered how their lips would blend—her softness and his hardness—came to fulfillment.

Her lips parted, letting his thrusting, searching tongue have its way, and she felt his palms on her back moving her hips against his, pressing the length of her body against his own.

A door slammed in the apartment, and Jenny pulled herself away, twisting out of Massimo's grasp and steadying herself against the railing. Her breath came in gasps.

Massimo looked at her, a question in his eyes.

"No," Jenny said in a trembling voice. "This can't happen . . . It *won't* happen. I don't want you. I . . . I have work to do here. Simon . . . I've only just . . . It's not fair. I have work to do here."

Massimo nodded. "You have work to do. And it is too soon, perhaps. But it will happen, *cara* Jennifer. It can, and it will."

He smiled and turned toward the glass doors, striding into the apartment.

Jenny stood, her hands gripping the iron railing, staring blankly out at the view. With a conscious effort she slowed her breathing. The pulse in her neck quieted, and she put the backs of her hands to her cheeks, letting them cool her hot face. Finally she took a deep breath, let it out slowly, and turned back toward the apartment.

A delicate silver bell sounded inside. Dinner was ready.

Two men stood at the oval dining room table when Jenny entered. The second was a smaller, slightly softer version of Massimo Silvano. Massimo smiled at her, but Jenny avoided his eyes.

"Signorina," he said casually, as though nothing had happened, "this is my brother Luca. Luca, the *Signorina* Jennifer Armstrong."

The man standing opposite her bowed. His cheeks were fuller than his brother's, and there was a touch of red in each one just at the cheekbone. His eyes were wider, with more white showing, but, Jenny noticed, without the touch of gold. His hair, as black as Massimo's, fell over his forehead in a tousled shock. Although he was probably no more than five years younger than his brother, he seemed somehow generations apart, without Massimo's dark look of having suffered through many battles. He was coltish and earnest—a cherub, Jenny thought whimsically.

She looked at Luca and instinctively smiled.

"I was so happy to learn you were here," the young man said with a small frown of concern. "I sent a man to meet you at the station, but he said you were not on the train."

"Oh, I missed that train—I had trouble with taxis at the Milan airport. I'm so sorry—I should have thought to let you know. But *Madama* Fortuna was a little vague about the arrangements, and I wasn't sure... And then I met Massimo... met your brother on the next train, and he brought me here. I just didn't think—"

"Oh, it's nothing. Massimo has told me about your meeting." Luca still sounded concerned, and he stroked his chin lightly.

"It was just coincidence, meeting Massimo," Jenny said lamely. "We... we just happened to be in the same compartment, and we introduced ourselves."

Jenny stole a glance at Massimo. He was watching her, an amused expression on his face, apparently enjoying her vague sense of embarrassment. She pushed her hair back from her face defiantly.

Luca nodded, looking at Jenny with wide, clear eyes. *"Si*, Massimo has said." His broad smile returned. "And here you are. That is the important thing. Shall we sit down?"

He took a step toward Jenny's side of the table, clearly planning to help her with her chair, but Massimo was already behind her. Jenny sat down. Massimo's hands, holding the back of her chair, barely brushed her shoulders, but Jenny felt a tiny shock pass through her body at his touch, and she shivered.

"So, is everything all right? Your room is satisfactory?" Luca asked anxiously. Jenny looked across the table at him gratefully. Luca's every word, every gesture, seemed reassuring. His youthful openness left nothing hidden; there was no sharpness to him.

"Everything is wonderful," she replied. "The room is beautiful. I do want to thank you for inviting me to stay here—and of course your brother as well." She gave a cursory nod in Massimo's direction and turned back to Luca. "I'm especially grateful for the worktable," she said. "I assume you were responsible for that?"

The tiny spots of red on Luca's cheeks grew larger, and he hung his head in apparent embarrassment. "I am glad you find it useful," he said. Then he smiled at Jenny almost shyly. He reminded Jenny of eight-year-old Nino, sitting quietly at the kitchen table. The tension of her encounter with Massimo was rapidly dissipating in the face of Luca's uncomplicated charm.

The kitchen door swung open, and Rosa appeared with a platter of pasta, its distinctive green sauce and piquant aroma making it recognizable to Jenny from her earlier visit to the kitchen. *Pesto,* Rosa had called it—crushed basil leaves, pine nuts, olive oil, and Parmesan. She remembered with amusement Nino's solemn translation of Rosa's insistence that *pesto* could only be made properly here in Genoa, where the sea breeze caressed each basil plant with just the right amounts of salt and moisture.

Jenny breathed in the wonderful fragrance.

"You know *pesto?*" Massimo asked. Jenny looked at him directly for the first time since she had entered the dining room.

His tall frame was reflected in the glass doors behind him, which were now closed, and beyond Jenny could see the night sky and the stars hanging low over the city. Massimo's eyes reflected nothing more than a polite interest in his guest.

"Rosa was telling me about it while the children ate supper." She smiled and breathed in again. "It smells too good to be true."

She wound several strands of the wide, homemade *fettuccine* around her fork and slid it into her mouth.

"It's heaven!" she cried softly.

The two men laughed. Jenny glanced at Massimo, and she could see the faint gleam of gold in his eyes. She looked back at Luca. They were, she thought good-naturedly, damnably attractive—both of them. It almost wasn't fair.

Luca chatted for a while about Jenny's trip, then turned to his brother. "And how were your travels, Massimo? Was your visit to Milan successful?"

Massimo nodded. "Everything was fine," he replied. "The contract was signed, as we expected."

Luca continued to chew his pasta. "And *cara* Miriam?" he asked casually. "She is fine also?"

Jenny felt an inner chill. She glanced at Massimo. His face seemed suddenly darker, like the sky when thunderclouds begin to gather.

"Miriam is fine, Luca," he said, his voice ominously soft. "Miriam and Carlo both."

Jenny blinked and looked intently at her food. Carlo? It was as though the brothers were talking in code, communicating in terms only they could understand.

"They would like to see you sometime, Luca," Massimo went on.

Jenny frowned at her plate.

"Ah," Luca murmured. "And of course I would like to see them." He was smiling but looking a little embarrassed, as though the conversation had taken a turn not quite to his liking. "But my commitments here are so difficult..."

Jenny looked quickly from one brother to the other. Massimo's face was masklike, utterly without emotion. Just what, she wondered, was Miriam to him? And who was Carlo? Luca was looking at her with his wide, earnest smile.

"There is always so much to do," he said with a shrug.

"And you, Jenny—you will be working with the enchanting Gabriella. You have met her? In New York perhaps?"

Jenny shook her head. "No, but I've admired her work for years, ever since I began designing myself." The coldness invading her began to disappear as she revealed her excitement over Gabriella and the new career opportunity she had been offered. Once again she felt grateful to Luca, whose open manner seemed to make tension melt away.

Rosa pushed open the door again and removed the pasta plates, replacing them with platters of thinly sliced veal swimming in butter and lemon and tender enough to be cut with a fork.

"I'm thrilled to be working with *Madama* Fortuna—Gabriella," Jenny concluded, letting the exquisite taste of the delicate veal seep into her senses.

Luca nodded enthusiastically. "She is wonderful to work with. A little temperamental, perhaps, but then, she is an artist!"

"Gabriella is temperamental only with those who do not meet her standards," Massimo said sharply. "I'm sure that Jenny will get along with her very well."

Luca looked at his brother for a moment, seeming to weigh his remark. Then he smiled and nodded. Jenny wondered at his equilibrium in the face of what seemed like goading from his brother.

"I am sure you are right, Massimo. She and Jenny will get along very well." Luca looked back at Jenny and winked. "You know that Gabriella is our friend, Massimo's and mine, almost since we were born. Of course, she is more Massimo's age. The two of them, they used to play together, bathe together . . . they were always together. In fact, our *mamma* has always felt that a match between Gabriella and one of us would be—what shall I say?—the perfect end to things. She was most unhappy when Massimo found his wife elsewhere."

He shook his head in mock solemnity. "And now that he is free again, well . . ."

Jenny looked quickly at Massimo. His eyes were almost closed, but there was a smile of amusement on his lips. She felt a twinge of real anger. How many women did he toy with at one time? Was it all a big game—keeping on some kind of string not only the fragile, pretty woman in Milan but also Gabriella Fortuna? And as if that weren't enough to satisfy him, to make a play for his new houseguest as well?

She pointedly turned back to Luca. "And what about you, Luca?" she asked teasingly. "Why don't *you* marry Gabriella?"

Luca's cheeks flamed. "Oh, I . . ." he stammered. "She is older than I, really, and my work . . . I keep so busy . . ."

From the end of the table Massimo laughed dryly, and Jenny shot a disapproving look at him. She nibbled on the fresh pear that Rosa had set in front of her.

"Do you work in the family business, too, Luca? Banking, I think Massimo said?"

"*Si,* we work together," Massimo interrupted before his brother had a chance to reply. "Banking."

Then he rose to his feet. "Luca, the *signorina* has had a difficult trip and has been up for many hours. She is certainly tired. I think we should be polite enough to let her go to her room now."

He remained standing, his frame casting its impressive reflection against the glass doors, until Luca had risen, too. There was a hint of anxious concern on the younger man's even features.

"Jenny, forgive me. I chatter on, and of course you are tired." Then his face brightened. "Perhaps tomorrow I can find time to show you around Genoa, if you would like."

"That would be delightful," Jenny responded.

"You will be needed at the office, Luca," Massimo said flatly.

Luca looked at his brother with a frown, then smiled in resignation and nodded.

"In any case," he said amiably to Jenny, "I am sure I will see you tomorrow sometime. Have a good rest." Then, with a little bow in Massimo's direction, he turned and left the room. A moment later, Jenny heard the apartment door close softly.

She glared at Massimo. "You certainly do enjoy giving people orders, don't you? Telling them when they must work and when they must go to bed..."

He looked at her steadily. "You are exhausted," he said.

"I am quite capable of deciding when I'm exhausted!" she snapped. But as she rose angrily to her feet, she realized just how right he was. Her legs were rubbery beneath her, and she grasped at the back of her chair for support. Massimo stepped quickly around the table and took her arm. He smiled down at her.

"Luca needs to go to work tomorrow," he said softly, "and you need to go to bed. Right now."

"I can do that alone," she said defiantly, pushing at her hair with her free hand.

He laughed. "Don't worry, *signorina*. I don't intend to take advantage of you. I like my women wide awake."

"Full of life," Jenny said.

"Full of life," he agreed.

Still holding her arm, Massimo led Jenny firmly back through the apartment to the door of her room. There they stood facing one another in the dimly lit hall. Exhaustion and not a little wine had dulled her senses, but Jenny was still annoyingly conscious of the well-made shape before her...the broad shoulders and chest, the slender waist and hips.

Massimo had taken off his tie earlier in the evening, and his jacket hung loose now. The white of his shirt gleamed in the shadowy hall, and Jenny felt an almost irresistible desire to reach forward and touch that whiteness, to slip her hand beneath it and stroke the hard flesh of his chest . . . It had been years since she'd felt this kind of physical urgency about a man.

"*Cara* Jenny," Massimo began softly. Then his voice was suddenly firmer. "I want you to understand something."

She looked at him, trying to concentrate on his voice, but her senses were filled with the look and smell of him. She knew, despite the strength of her anger with him, that if he reached for her now she could not, would not, resist.

"Things are not always exactly as they seem," he was saying. "Luca, for instance . . ."

Jenny blinked, forcing her eyes wide and making herself hear what he was saying. She had not expected a discussion about Luca.

"Luca is charming, no? You find him appealing. He does not . . . I think the word is threaten. He does not threaten you."

Jenny nodded, confused. "He's a very nice boy," she said, her tongue feeling slightly thick.

Massimo shook his head gravely. "Luca is not a boy," he said. "One must have some care . . . one must be . . . a little careful."

Jenny straightened with one fierce shudder and pulled her arm away from Massimo's hand.

"Are you suggesting that I need protection from your brother?" she asked angrily.

Massimo smiled and shrugged. "Perhaps protection is too strong a word."

"If I need protection from anyone in this house," she snapped furiously, "it's not from Luca. It's from you!"

Jenny pushed the door of her room open and swung it sharply shut behind her. She leaned back, letting her tired body rest along the length of it. For a moment there was silence in the hallway, and then she heard Massimo's footsteps, light but sharp, moving quickly away.

Chapter 3

IT WAS ALMOST ten o'clock when Jenny opened her eyes the next morning. She lay back against the soft pillows for a moment, her fingers toying absently with the satiny coverlet, and let her gaze range about the elegant room. A frown creased her forehead. It *was* lovely here, and comfortable, but she would have to leave. She had no doubt, not after last night: living here would be impossible.

With a little sigh, she swung her legs over the side of the bed and padded to the bathroom, her bare toes sinking into the thick, luxurious pile of the Persian carpets with each step.

It really was unfair to be confronted with Massimo Silvano five weeks after she had freed herself from Simon. There was no doubt about her attraction to Massimo. Even now, as she rubbed at her face with a fluffy washcloth, she could feel a tiny knot form in her stomach when she pictured his face, his chestnut eyes, and the dark, slashing eyebrows.

Jenny returned to the bedroom and studied her small wardrobe critically. Yellow sun peeped through the cracks of the interior shutters that covered her room's only window, and she pulled one of them open to see what kind of day it was. The window faced the street and was sealed shut, with heavy bars protecting it on the outside. A sardonic smile tugged at the corners of Jenny's mouth. The apartment she had shared with Simon had been an emotional cage, but this was a real one: luxurious and tempting, but a cage nevertheless, with bars on the windows and a dangerous guard just beyond the door. Somehow the notion amused her.

She pulled on tan gabardine slacks and a soft, royal-blue jersey blouse. Wrapping her thick hair around two fingers, she pinned it quickly into something resembling a bun at the nape of her neck. Several wispy tendrils refused to be imprisoned, and they feathered softly about her face. She brushed a touch of blue onto her eyelids and left her naturally pink cheeks without makeup. It wouldn't be long, she thought with pleasure, before this brilliant sun would turn her ivory skin a nice golden brown.

Jenny assumed that the apartment would be almost empty at this hour—the children would be at school and Massimo and Luca at work. Only Rosa would be on hand to help with breakfast, and with her lack of English and Jenny's limited grasp of Italian, there wouldn't be much conversation. Jenny picked up her Italian tourist office guide to Genoa to read at the breakfast table.

But the apartment was not empty. As Jenny pushed open the door from the kitchen to the dining room, holding the cup of steaming coffee that Rosa had thrust into her hand, Massimo looked up from his newspaper and nodded to her. He was sitting where he had the night before, at the far end of the table, with his back to the glass terrace doors.

"*Buon giorno,* Jenny," he said politely. "Did you sleep well?" He smiled with his mouth, but his eyes were impassive. He folded the newspaper and laid it on the table beside a small silver pot of coffee.

Jenny's hand trembled slightly as she put her own coffee cup down, and she felt a quick burst of anger at her body. Why was it that her hands seemed to have a life of their own, to respond to stimuli against all her wishes? She sat down and folded the misbehaving hands in her lap for a moment, forcing a polite smile onto her face.

"Yes, thank you, very well. The room is very comfortable." A small sip of coffee burned as it slid down her throat, and she dismissed the thought of last night's scene with Massimo from her mind as quickly as it appeared. "It's late," she went on. "I hope you weren't waiting for me—I should have gotten up sooner."

Massimo shook his head, and his smile broadened. "Not at all. I often work at home. But today I am not working at all."

Jenny's eyebrows rose questioningly, and Massimo tilted his head as if in an answering nod. "You must have a guide to Genoa today, no?"

Jenny felt the muscles of her jaw tighten as her teeth clenched. Rosa opened the kitchen door, and both Jenny and Massimo watched her deposit a large tray on the table in front of Jenny. On it was a tempting array of scrambled eggs, thinly sliced ham, warm bread, tiny crocks of butter and jam, a tall, icy glass of almost red orange juice, and a small pitcher of hot milk. Jenny looked at the food with undeniable interest, and then shifted her attention back to Massimo.

"Actually, I was planning to explore on my own," she said.

Massimo shook his head seriously. "I think not. Genoa is beautiful and inviting, but it is also a port. If you don't know your way about, especially a young woman alone . . ." He shrugged and let his words trail off.

Jenny could see the soft gleam of gold in his eyes, and behind him the bright, lemon-yellow of the morning sun shone through the glass doors, forming a hazy aura around his dark head. Jenny felt a tiny quickening of her pulse.

She shook her head fiercely, remembering when she had first arrived in New York. She recalled how Simon, confident and handsome, had shaped her fears of the big city, had played on her naiveté and made himself indispensable to her.

"You forget that I've lived in New York for eight years," she said briskly. "I can take care of myself." She speared some egg and ham with her fork, popped it into her mouth, and chewed determinedly.

Massimo watched her for a moment. Then, with a little sigh, he turned his chair slightly and looked out toward the electric-blue Mediterranean sky.

"I have no doubt of that," he said. "I do not mean to intrude on your independence. Believe me, I have learned long ago that women will do as they wish."

There was something resigned, even weary, about his voice that made Jenny look up from the bread she was buttering. His eyes were tired, and there was a hint of remembered pain in them. The gold had disappeared. Jenny blinked at her sudden remembrance of his mouth against hers, the sweet taste of his tongue as it had touched her own. She was confused.

"I would enjoy showing you Genoa," Massimo went on. "I love it, and I know it well." He spread his hands in the air, palms upward, in a gesture of supplication— and one that seemed to say that these hands hid no tricks.

Jenny chewed thoughtfully, savoring the homemade raspberry jam. Her apartment could wait at least a day— and it *did* make sense to have a thorough tour of the city. What harm could it do, really, to spend a day with Massimo?

She nodded and smiled. "Okay. I suspect you'll be better than my book." She waved her bread at the tourist office guide that lay next to her plate.

Massimo returned her smile, his teeth strong and white against his dark skin, and she remembered the way he had looked at the Milan station the day before: remote and elegant in his pinstripe suit. She saw again that first dazzling smile that had transformed his face into something open and vulnerable; and she felt again that slight rubbery sensation in her legs, her first acknowledgment that he was extraordinarily handsome. She was grateful that she was sitting down.

Jenny finished her breakfast as Massimo sipped his *caffè latte*—coffee laced with steamed milk—and quickly sketched for her the history of Genoa. His face glowed with animation as he described the long periods of strength and wealth his city had enjoyed before Italy had become a nation—times when Genoa had vied with Venice and Parma for supremacy on the seas. He told her about the bloody controversies among the great Genovese families, and about the canny business sense of many of those same families. Jenny watched his face, fascinated by the play of intelligence and pride in eyes that more often hid all emotion.

"There was a time when everyone came to Genoa," Massimo explained. "Especially the *Americani,* because it is the birthplace of Christopher Columbus." Massimo leaned back in his chair, laced his fingers behind his head, and fixed his eyes on the crystal chandelier. "But your Mark Twain had a different reason for appreciating it. 'There may be prettier women in Europe, but I doubt it,' he said. He thought it would be impossible for an ordinary man to marry here, because before he could make up his mind, he would fall in love with somebody else."

Jenny glanced at Massimo and laughed. "Well, Mark Twain is never wrong," she said. "So how about you and Luca? You've married once, but Luca never has. Is he afflicted with Mark Twain's disease?"

Massimo grinned. "Luca, ah . . ." He looked at the

ceiling again and shook his head. "Luca falls in love continually. He cannot help himself; it is, as you say, a disease."

Jenny pursed her lips. Was it this simple message that Massimo had been trying to convey last night—that Luca's affections were easily, but only temporarily, engaged?

"But I . . ." Massimo went on, his eyes wide and golden, "I am not an ordinary man. I do not readily fall in love. Only once in my life."

He caught Jenny's eyes and refused to let them go. Her cheeks felt warm, and she wondered if their pink was now red. She fiddled absently with the knot of hair at the nape of her neck.

"Or perhaps twice," he added softly.

Jenny looked away as two images flashed through her mind. The first was Massimo's wife, the classically beautiful woman whose picture on the piano showed her holding the two Silvano children, her face cool and emotionless. The second was the pale, fragile woman whom Jenny had glimpsed at the Milan station and again in the painfully private photo in the Silvano living room. Miriam.

Massimo pushed his chair away from the table. "Well," he said lightly, "perhaps you would like to see the beauties of Genoa for yourself now. Both the city and its women."

Jenny wiped her mouth with her napkin and folded it carefully beside her now-empty plate. "I'd like that."

Genoa was everything Massimo had promised it would be. And Massimo was an enchanting guide—knowledgeable, amusing, full of lovely, odd bits of gossip and history.

Jenny was conscious of the skill and strength of his hands as he maneuvered the silver-gray Fiat through wide boulevards and tiny alleyways, along elegant shopping streets, past the ruin of the opera house that had been bombed in the war and never rebuilt, and the small stone house that now stood where Columbus had grown up. She laughed as he pointed out the hideous excesses of the great bank buildings that surrounded *Piazza De Ferrari* at the center of town.

Massimo drove slowly down *Via Garibaldi*, the Street of Palaces, where the wealthy families of fifteenth-century Genoa had built their massive, thick-walled homes. It was now, Massimo explained, the city's center, but then it had been suburbia—outside the original city walls. He pulled the car to a halt in front of one of the imposing *palazzi* and pointed to a brass plaque beside the open gates: SOCIETÀ SILVANO.

"This is our office," he said. Jenny peered out the window at the great building. Through the gates she could see a small cobbled yard where several cars were parked, and beyond, through a second set of gates, was another, larger courtyard, lush and green with flowering shrubs and a small fountain at its center. The *palazzo* itself was built around the garden.

"It's remarkable!" she cried.

Massimo nodded. "They are all like that." He gestured at the other palaces that lined the street. "They were built for two things: on the outside, defense; on the inside, comfort and tranquillity. The walls are thick, virtually impenetrable. But inside there is life, sunlight, luxury even." He looked at Jenny and smiled slyly. "Once Gabriella Fortuna told me I was like one of these Renaissance *palazzi*. Very strong defenses on the outside, but full of surprises—delights, perhaps—for those who could penetrate my walls."

Massimo continued to look at Jenny, a hint of amusement in his gold-rimmed eyes. She gave him what she hoped was a cool smile. She wondered briefly just how much Gabriella Fortuna—and heaven knew how many other women—had tasted of those delights. She felt once again the stirring deep inside her that Massimo seemed so capable of exciting.

"I don't think I'll attack just yet," she said dryly. "I'm not sure I'm ready for the unexpected."

Massimo's slashing eyebrows rose. "You are so certain, then, that you could breach my defenses?"

Jenny laughed lightly. "Your defenses don't seem so strong to me." She turned to look at the *palazzo* again. "Not nearly as strong as those walls, anyway."

Massimo nodded in mock gravity. "Perhaps not. Sometimes, of course, the *conte* or *principe* rode out from his palace and simply took what he wanted—land, money, a woman. At those times, defenses played no role at all. No one could defend against those men."

Jenny shot a glance at Massimo's sharp profile with its long nose and high forehead, the heavy-lidded eyes, and the thick black hair. She didn't doubt his lineal connection with those counts and princes of the Renaissance. What he wanted, he would take. She took in a deep breath and let it out slowly, every nerve alert to his closeness.

"That was then," she said, "and now is now. Women are no longer simply there for the taking."

Massimo laughed. "No," he agreed. "Sometimes now it is the women who take." Jenny blinked at the bitterness in his voice.

Finally Massimo swung the car around the train station where they had arrived the previous day and into the dark, narrow alleys along the waterfront. They drove slowly along the cobbled street that ran parallel to the docks. To their left ran the low stone portico of the original marketplace. Burly men wandered beneath it, some straining under the weight of wooden cartons filled with fish, some just talking and smoking. Jenny could smell the salty odor of fish and a hint of garbage.

To their right were the great docks themselves, wood, stone, and steel structures that seemed to extend for miles out to sea. Along them were ranged the massive ships Jenny had seen from the terrace the night before. From the distance they had seemed like toys; now, as Massimo parked in front of one of the gleaming white liners, the ships loomed above them, bigger than she had ever imagined.

"Farther west, toward the airport," Massimo explained, "there are modern docks and an oil pipeline that allows the precious liquid to be unloaded directly from the great tankers. But these are the docks on which Genoa was founded; the stones of these piers were here when the Doria warships sailed for Venice."

Jenny watched Massimo as he talked. She could see again in his face the history of those families—their arrogance and their courage. She could see the centuries of cleverness that had kept Genoa Europe's largest port.

Instinctively, she touched his sleeve with her hand. Massimo turned abruptly to face her, as if awakened from a daydream. He smiled and gestured behind her.

"The sea looks less romantic by day, I fear, than it does from our terrace by night."

Jenny turned her head reluctantly, not really wanting to look away from that dark, angular face. The water where it lapped at the base of the liner was dirty brown, with bottles, boxes, and trash floating in it. She turned back to Massimo with a grimace.

"Why don't they clean it up?"

He shrugged. "Too expensive. And no need. No one swims here, or drinks the water. And the smell doesn't carry too far." His eyes, the lids half-closed, were looking past Jenny toward the sea. Then suddenly they shifted back to her face. "I liked the feel of your hand on my arm," he said softly.

Massimo lifted his own hand from the wheel of the car and slid it beneath the hair caught up in its thick bun just above her collar. His fingers rested there lightly. They felt cool, but Jenny's skin felt hot and damp beneath them. She shifted uneasily in the seat.

"Massimo . . ." she said tentatively.

He shifted, too, turning his body slightly toward her and letting his other hand drop from the wheel onto her thigh. He stroked the rough gabardine delicately, his thumb barely grazing the inner seam of her slacks. Jenny felt a shudder of excitement race through her body at his touch. Where his hands rested, her flesh felt alive and vibrant—suddenly full of its own energies. A glorious warmth flooded those two small patches of flesh, and Jenny wondered urgently what the rest of her body would feel like, touched by his strong fingers.

Jenny's eyes fell to the dark, smooth triangle at the base of Massimo's throat, where his soft white shirt fell open. She watched the tiny, irregular pulse that beat there as if it were something apart from them both.

Then, almost as if in a dream, she bent her head forward and pressed her mouth to the warm flesh, feeling it tighten beneath her lips, feeling the same kind of excitement flood through Massimo that was overwhelming her own body. Her shoulders straightened, as if with a will of their own, arching her full, rounded breasts toward him.

Massimo's breath was heavy and slightly labored as he slid his hand around her throat and under her chin, lifting her head from his chest. His lips closed over hers, and a soft moan escaped her as she opened her mouth to his, inviting the sweet warmth of his tongue to taste her own.

Jenny's own breath quickened. It had been like this with Simon briefly, for that first month or two. She had felt this same kind of urgent, almost frantic need for him.

Massimo's fingers moved downward, brushing the creamy column of her throat and catching in the V of her soft blouse. He began to undo the top button with an unhurried clarity of movement, as if they were underwater...or in a dream. His fingers touched the wisp of fabric that held her full breasts, then slid inside it, tentatively at first and then with increasing pressure. He

held the heaviness of her breasts, first one and then the
other, in his strong hand, kneading, stroking. The warm,
firm flesh responded to his touch, the dark centers hard-
ening beneath his fingers. Jenny's breath came in tiny,
shallow gasps.

Massimo's mouth clung to hers with a hunger that
seemed to echo her own. She moved her tongue against
his teeth, wanting to feel their hardness, and his hand,
still gentle on her leg, moved upward in response. He
pressed lightly against her warmth, and Jenny heard a
tiny cry that she knew had come from her own throat.
She pulled him more tightly against her, crushing the
firm flesh of her breasts against his chest, holding his
hand captive where it explored beneath her blouse.

From somewhere behind Massimo she heard a voice,
deep, harsh, and intrusive. Massimo jerked his head away
and turned. There was a face at the window of the car,
a dark face with a cigar dangling from the corner of its
mouth, and the face was saying something in rough, rapid
Italian. Massimo glared at the man for a moment, his
eyes glowing like coals, then relaxed slightly. He moved
his hands away from Jenny, resting one on the wheel
and one on the back of the seat, then said something to
the man. The face laughed, took a long, amused look at
Jenny, and moved away.

"We can't park here," Massimo said lightly. "They
need to get cargo through."

Jenny leaned back against the seat of the car and
breathed deeply, letting her frantic excitement slowly
subside. Her fingers fumbled at the buttons of her blouse
and pushed at her errant hair, adjusting and arranging.

As Massimo twisted the key in the ignition of the car,
she glanced at his face. It held an expression of casual
amusement. His breath came evenly, and a small smile
played at the corners of his mouth. Jenny stared at him.
It had taken him only a moment to recover his compo-
sure—from an encounter that Jenny knew would remain

with her for a long time to come.

The man with the cigar stood across the street, still laughing, as they pulled away.

"What did you say to him?" Jenny asked, suddenly feeling a tinge of embarrassment coloring her cheeks.

Massimo shrugged. "Just an old Genovese saying about the needs of the flesh erupting at the most awkward moments."

"Is . . . is that all you felt?" Jenny asked softly, feeling the red warmth in her cheeks spread down her throat. "Some physical . . . need . . . ?"

Massimo looked at her, his face no longer amused. "Really, Jenny," he said sharply. "Let's not be children."

Jenny blinked as though he had slapped her.

"So," he went on, turning the car away from the waterfront. "Shall we have some lunch? I know a very nice place in *centro*—the old city—and we haven't really looked around there yet."

Jenny turned away from him. The morning had been so lovely, and Massimo so delightful. She had begun to let herself believe he was different, that he was not another self-centered, flirtatious Simon interested only in fulfilling some obscure need of his own by making a play for every woman who walked by. But he wasn't different at all. Men, she thought with a sudden bitterness, never really were.

He had even been honest with her: I don't fall in love, he had said. I have very strong defenses. And what I want, I take.

Well, I can build defenses, too, Jenny thought fiercely. The next time *signore* Silvano decides he wants *this* lady, he's going to find a stone wall in his way!

But even as she made her private vow, Jenny could feel the warmth of his fingertips against her skin, the taste of his tongue as it explored her mouth. The dusky flesh at the center of her breasts hardened again at the memory, and she shifted her hips against the soft upholstery. She stared grimly out the window of the car. A small tear worked its way out of the corner of her eye, sliding gently down her cheek, and she raised a finger angrily to brush it away.

Massimo circled around the historical district to the center of town and parked the car on a side street off *Piazza De Ferrari*. Jenny let him take her arm and guide her back into the maze of tiny streets that was the original city. She willed her flesh not to respond to his touch.

A cool calm settled over her as they made their way along the narrow streets, some only ten or twelve feet wide, between equally narrow buildings that rose abruptly from the edges of the cobbled streets. Women leaned out of windows three and four stories up to string laundry between the buildings and exchange gossip in raucous tones.

Once their progress was interrupted by a small crowd that had gathered around two mangy cats, one with a missing ear, who were circling one another and hissing, their backs arched menacingly. Massimo found a path around the edge of the group, but as they walked on Jenny could hear the angry howl of the cats as they finally joined in battle, and the mocking, unpleasant laughter of the crowd.

Massimo talked easily about the area as they walked. Jenny's angry calm, the coolness she had forced on herself, slowly began to dissolve; there was, she had to admit, a charming, little-boy pride in Massimo's attitude toward his beloved city that appealed to her. His sense of tradition and roots brought with it something solid and stable, something that contrasted sharply with Simon's nervous concentration on current fashions. She would have to take care, she told herself; it was almost amusing how quickly she could lose sight of Massimo's casual, arrogant attitude toward women.

Down a side street Jenny glimpsed two men circling each other in the same menacing way the cats had, but before she could comment, Massimo had stopped in front of an ordinary-looking building, its single window blocked by a dusty red curtain, and gestured Jenny inside. There were two small rooms, each with three or four tables covered by snowy cloths and set with unmatched glass- and silverware. By the door was a small table, from which a fat, dark woman rose excitedly when they entered.

"Signore Silvano!" she cried. *"E troppo tempo— troppo, troppo!"* She wrapped thick arms around Massimo in a bear hug, then dropped them almost immediately to her sides and stepped back shyly.

"Buon giorno, Sofia," he said warmly. "It *has* been too long. And this," he went on, gesturing at Jenny, "is my new friend from America. *Mi'amica Americana nuova.* Jennifer Armstrong, Sofia Traverso."

The woman grinned and shook Jenny's hand energetically for a long moment. Her eyes swept critically from the top of Jenny's head to the floor and back up again. Apparently satisfied, she dropped Jenny's hand with a wink and quick remark to Massimo that Jenny didn't understand and led them to a corner table.

A moment later, Sofia deposited a big basket of warm bread and a crock of butter on their table and filled their glasses from an unlabeled bottle of red wine. She brought menus, but Massimo waved them away.

"You will let me order for you?" he asked, almost as an afterthought. Jenny nodded, thinking wryly that that was one decision she was willing to have him make for her.

Massimo said a few words to Sofia, who then scurried off, disappearing behind a beaded curtain at the back of the room.

Jenny felt a stirring in her stomach which, this time,

had nothing whatever to do with the attraction she felt for the man sitting opposite her. She was hungry. It was, she realized, almost three in the afternoon. A smile settled on her lips as she waited for their food to arrive.

"This is one of my favorite restaurants in all of Genoa," Massimo said. "When I was a boy, my father used to bring me here for lunch—it's an easy walk from the *Società* offices. Sofia's mamma ran things then. Now she and her husband are in charge. I hope you're hungry."

Jenny nodded enthusiastically. If he wanted to behave as though nothing had happened between them, it was a game she could play as well. "Starving!" she affirmed.

She let her gaze range around the unpretentious room, then turned back to Massimo. "Did you often go to the office with your father?"

Massimo shrugged. "I was the oldest son. I was expected to learn the business—and learn it well. Yes, I was there quite often."

Jenny nodded. "And Luca? Was he expected to learn, too?"

Massimo's face darkened slightly. "Luca, no. He was not greatly interested, and since I was..." He left the sentence unfinished. "And you? Did your father wish you to enter his business?" His eyes were amused as he watched her.

Jenny laughed at the thought. "My father left my mother when I was barely six," she said. "I hardly even remember him." She pursed her lips slightly at the flashing vision of a face full of laughter, a shock of carroty hair.

Massimo looked at her sharply. But whatever he might have said was lost; Sofia arrived at that moment bearing bowls of aromatic *pasta primavera*—springtime pasta, with a thin, cream and butter sauce and a rich collection of crisp vegetables tucked into it.

The conversation stayed on the safer ground of history

as they worked their way through the pasta and then through delicately broiled fillets of some red fish that Jenny couldn't identify. It seemed to her that she hardly sipped her wine at all, but the level in the bottle moved lower and lower, and her face had taken on a glowing warmth.

"*Centro* is my favorite part of the city," Massimo was saying thoughtfully as they nibbled at the light, flaky dessert pastries Sofia had brought out as a special treat. "So full of life. But of course it is still the waterfront. There are many..." He lifted his eyes and shoulders searchingly. "Rough types. Both men and women." He smiled at Jenny. "One does not wander alone without knowing the way."

Jenny's eyes widened. She tossed her head, shaking the hair that had worked its way loose from her bun away from her face.

"It seems to me that we've had this conversation before," she said, bristling. "And it seems to me that I told you at breakfast that I'm quite capable of taking care of myself—under *any* conditions."

Massimo shook his head slowly, his eyes on her face. "Jenny, Jenny," he said. "You are so easily insulted. This husband of yours, he must have..." He let his words trail off, then folded his hands on the table. "In *centro* it is not simply a matter of taking care of oneself. People get drunk here at all hours of the day. There are some areas where men assume that every woman is fair game."

"Perhaps they're not used to women who are *not* fair game, and who will fight for their rights."

Massimo laughed softly. "What are a woman's rights against a knife, Jenny? No." He shook his head again. "All your talk about independence and taking care of yourself would matter little here. A woman needs a man here. To fight for her."

"There are very few things I need a man for, Massimo." Jenny's voice was almost hoarse with the anger she felt welling up inside. How many times had she had this argument with Simon; how many times had he insisted to her that women could not function on their own, without men to guide them and explain? How many times had he used that as an excuse for his relationships with other women—women who *needed* him?

"In fact," she continued, "at the moment I can only think of one thing that I'd need a man for, and I'm not altogether sure I really need that. I've lived without it fairly successfully for quite a while."

Massimo laughed in genuine amusement. "No woman can do without *that*, my little tigress—and you, from what I've experienced in the last twenty-four hours, least of all."

Jenny felt such a great flood of anger and embarrassment at his words that it left her speechless; her hands clenched in her lap so hard that the nails bit into her palms.

Massimo put his elbows on the table and leaned forward, lowering his voice. "Perhaps you've just not had the proper man to teach you. We men who are good at it must be careful whom we select to teach, because once a woman has tasted *real* lovemaking, she sometimes finds it hard to stop." His words were teasing but hard, and his eyes were flat and opaque, without their golden glow. There was pain in his voice, but Jenny's anger let her dismiss it, leaving only the arrogance of his words.

She forced a calm smile onto her face and folded her napkin carefully beside her plate, smoothing it with both hands.

"You needn't concern yourself with teaching *me, signore* Silvano," she said softly. Her voice sounded harsh and tinny even to her own ears. "I've already learned several things from men in my life, and one of them is that I have nothing more to learn from men."

Massimo was about to respond when Sofia approached

the table with their check. He held up one finger to Jenny, as if to say that he would answer in a minute, then reached for his wallet as he glanced at the bill.

"It's been a lovely lunch, Massimo. Thank you." Determination welled through her body. "If you'll just excuse me for a moment, I'd like to freshen up."

Massimo pointed absently toward a door by the kitchen, then went back to counting out money. Jenny snatched her purse from the table and walked quickly to the front of the restaurant.

She hesitated only a brief moment in the street outside, then turned a corner and headed down what looked like a familiar passage. She smiled grimly as she walked—almost ran—and turned again almost immediately to evade Massimo's anticipated pursuit. She would find her way out of *centro,* she vowed furiously; she would *prove* to him that she could take care of herself. She had made her way home from Times Square to Greenwich Village countless times after the theater—how much worse could this possibly be?

She hurried on, barely noticing where she was going, wanting only to be away from Massimo and his patronizing, infuriating manner. The streets were lively, lined with shops and full of people. At every turning there seemed to be a church with broad front steps and the ancient, black or green and white striped marble facade that had become familiar to her in the day's touring. She wished she had the time and freedom to stop and explore.

Finally she did stop to catch her breath in a miniature *piazza.* A troop of ragged boys playing soccer off to one side stopped their game and hooted at her with good-natured leers. She avoided looking their way, focusing her attention instead on the various little alleyways that led off the *piazza.* It was time to begin making her way back toward the *Piazza De Ferrari* and the car.

She entered one of the streets tentatively. It was extremely narrow, perhaps eight feet wide, and there were no stores along it. The buildings on either side seemed closed and hostile, with no windows at street level and heavy locks on their wooden doors. The tall buildings blocked the waning afternoon sun; despite the early hour, darkness was beginning to close in. The sound of Jenny's footsteps echoed hollowly against the cobbled pavement, and there was a distinctive odor in the air—fish and salt-water and garbage. The waterfront. I'm going in the wrong direction, she thought abruptly—and for the first time, she felt a little shudder of fear.

The soft glow of a neon sign at the end of the street caught her eye. She moved ahead. All she really needed to know was the general direction of *Piazza De Ferrari*. She stepped into the bar beneath the sign.

The small room was packed with swarthy men, some in the scruffy outfits of merchant seamen, some in uniforms of various navies. With a sigh of relief, Jenny saw the distinctive cap of an American sailor at the back. The other men made no effort to part as she made her way toward the American, and she felt her body graze several others as she pushed past. She knew there was a red flush in her cheeks, and she heard muffled snickers behind her.

"Excuse me," she said when she finally reached her destination. "You're an American?"

The man, heavy-set and showing the beginnings of a dark beard, nodded.

"I am, too. I'm lost." She smiled at him brightly. "Could you point me in the right direction for *Piazza De Ferrari?*"

The man held a beer bottle in one hand. He had tattoos on both forearms; one, Jenny noted uncomfortably, was an eagle holding a dove in its sharp talons. He looked at her, moving his head slightly as though to focus his vision.

"Oh, baby's lost," he said in a tone of mock sympathy. "Poor baby." He lifted both hands off the bar and laid them on Jenny's shoulders. The beer bottle, still clutched in one, felt cold against her jersey shirt.

Jenny stepped back quickly, and the sailor's hands fell, brushing her breasts as he reached back for the bar to steady himself. Jenny's breath quickened in distaste. She took another step backward. A hand grasped her waist from behind, and she whirled around, pushing the hand away and striding quickly out of the bar. Laughter from within echoed in the afternoon gloom.

Jenny turned back down the narrow street in the direction from which she had come. In one of the doorways, now unlocked, stood three brassily dressed women, their eyes made up in outrageous hues. They watched her with blank hostility as she approached, and Jenny realized they were not women at all, but mere girls—not more than fourteen or fifteen years old. Instinctively, she quickened her steps back toward the little *piazza* where the boys were playing.

A church stood to one side of the open square. Jenny walked determinedly to the fountain in front of it and, leaning against it, pulled the tourist guide book from her purse with hands that were beginning to tremble. It hadn't occurred to her that she could get so lost so quickly in the maze of streets and alleys. Tears welled slowly in her eyes, and Jenny batted at them angrily with the back of one hand. *Damn* Massimo Silvano, she thought fiercely. If he had just let her be, instead of challenging her with his arrogant warnings...

Tears blurred her vision as she flipped through the book's map section, and she groped in her purse for a tissue, holding the book under one elbow. Rage and frustration came together as the guide book slipped into the little stone fountain. It was easily retrievable, but it was already soaked through. With an exclamation of anger, Jenny fished it out and shook it sharply, sending little droplets of water in every direction.

It was possible, she admitted to herself for the first time, that it was all a mistake. And not simply this little adventure in *centro,* but the whole thing. Giving up her job in New York, coming to Genoa . . . maybe even leaving Simon. Maybe what Simon and Massimo believed was true: maybe she *did* need a man to look after her, to tell her what to do and how to do it. She leaned heavily back against the fountain, the soggy book limp in her hand.

She looked around the *piazza.* The boys had stopped their soccer game and were huddled together, whispering and glancing her way. Jenny took a deep breath and blew it out slowly. Then she straightened her shoulders, pushed her hair off her face, and started toward them. This was, after all, no time for regrets. The immediate problem was to get out of *centro.*

From the corner of her eye she saw a flash of navy-blue and white. She turned her head. The American sailor, beer bottle still in hand, was lurching into the *piazza.* Jenny quickened her steps. The boys seemed considerably less threatening than the lone adult male. She reached the edge of their huddle just as the sailor reached her.

"So, baby still lost?" he asked, his words slurring.

Jenny ignored him. *"Scusi, prego,"* she said to the boys. *"Dov'è Piazza De Ferrari?"*

The group parted slightly, enough to let Jenny advance a step of two into their midst. With wide brown eyes the boys looked back and forth from Jenny to the sailor.

"Hey, lady, I'm talkin' to you," the American said, now clearly belligerent. He reached out a hand and laid it on her shoulder, turning her toward him.

Jenny turned abruptly on her own. "Get your hands off me," she snapped, her voice low and defiant. Anger brought with it a surge of renewed confidence.

The sailor laughed and reached out again, this time grasping Jenny around the waist. She pulled back, but

she couldn't shake the hand loose. The boys spoke in
hushed voices, and then one took a step forward, his
brow creased in a frown.

"Signore, ferma, prego," he began, *"la signorina ..."*

But the sailor paid no attention. Jenny felt her knees
give slightly as the big man pulled her toward him. His
other hand went around her waist and felt heavy and
damp against her side. She had a brief, irrational vision
of her good gabardine slacks spattered with beer. The
bottle slipped from the man's hand and shattered on the
cobbled pavement, sending glass and beer splashing across
the stones.

"Haven't seen a good-looking American woman for
months," the sailor muttered as his hands kneaded Jenny's waist.

She turned to the boys. *"Prego,"* she said as she
pushed at the sailor's thick wrists. *"La polizia ..."*

One of the boys left the group and took off at a run
down a side street.

Jenny turned back to the American. "Get your filthy
hands off me," she cried, her voice full of rage. She
aimed a toe at his shin and kicked hard, but still his
meaty hands held on, and his watery, unfocused eyes
moved closer and closer. Jenny felt tears of frustration
and horror blur her own vision.

Then suddenly he had let go.

Strong, copper-colored hands held the white uniform
by the shoulders. The sailor stumbled backward, his mouth
open. The familiar hands swung the American around,
holding him upright.

"Hey, buster," he began, raising one arm as if to
swing. But Massimo swatted the arm away.

"Get out of my sight. Now." Massimo's voice was
sharp and brutal, like the edge of a knife.

The sailor looked him over, taking in the size and

supple strength of Massimo's body. Then he looked away.

"Didn't mean nothin'.," he muttered. "Didn't know the lady already had a boyfriend."

Massimo's eyes burned like hot coals, and the lines in his cheeks seemed etched by acid. Jenny stared at Massimo's face, seeing in it a viciousness that surprised and frightened her.

"Get out of here," he said again. *"Subito."*

The sailor raised his hands. "Didn't mean no harm," he continued to mutter as he stumbled out of the *piazza* and back toward the bar.

Jenny felt her whole body shake as Massimo turned toward her. His face was expressionless, like a mask carved from stone, and his hand closed on her arm like a vise.

"You fool," he spat. "Of all the stupid stunts. *Sai pazza*—you're insane!"

Jenny's eyes studied the cobbled pavement. The pressure of his hand around her arm was painful. She felt an overwhelming relief at his presence—but also a tinge of annoyance. There was no need for him to chide her as if she were a child. Her chin jutted out as she touched the shattered glass with the toe of one shoe.

"I could have worked things out for myself," she said defiantly, her eyes still on the cobblestones.

Massimo's laugh was quick and sharp. "Of course. You might have lectured him about the rights of women and bored him into submission."

"The boys had gone for a policeman." Jenny looked up. Massimo was glaring at her, his eyes opaque without a hint of gold. There was no warmth in them, only a fierce, frightening electricity that came spitting out at her as if from a broken live wire.

"And once you had dispensed with your boyfriend," he went on, "you might have used your little guide book to march out of this jungle." He gestured contemptuously at the wet book that now lay abandoned on the pavement amidst the beer and broken glass.

Tears started again, and Jenny fought them desperately. Her lower lip was trembling, and she felt the warmth of a deep red flush in her cheeks. She blinked hard, willing the tears not to fall.

"I could have—" she began again.

But suddenly Massimo's arms were around her, pulling her to him, and his mouth was closing over her own in a hard, bruising kiss. He twined one hand in the thick knot of hair at the back of her neck, forcing her lips tighter against his. She tried to pull away, pushing urgently at his chest, but she could not. The sweet taste of his mouth mingled with the salt of her tears.

His other hand sought the small of her back and arched her hips against his, as if trying fiercely to meld their bodies together. She could feel the hardness of him pressing against the base of her belly. She couldn't breath.

His need for her seemed desperate, and the kiss, a punishment; yet Jenny felt a primitive response in her own body, a yearning that reached toward Massimo and answered his need in kind. She slid her hands beneath his jacket, kneading the hard, muscular flesh of his sides and back through his shirt, and she moved against him. A wave of sensation shot through her breasts as they were crushed against his chest.

The sound of a wolf whistle startled them both. As Massimo released Jenny, the boys who still stood surrounding them took up a rhythmic applause, stomping their feet and whistling in approval.

Jenny gasped for breath. She instinctively reached a hand to her hair, which had come loose from its bun and now hung in a tangled mass below her shoulders. Massimo glared at the boys with a cold violence that silenced them; then, as he took in their pleased, shy grins, his face relaxed and he smiled back. He ducked his head in a nod, acknowledging their applause.

"Grazie, ragazzi," he said. *"Una lezione d'amore . . ."*

He let his hand slide down Jenny's arm to her elbow. "Come, *cara mia*. We should go home now."

Jenny nodded. She felt drained of all energy, almost of all life. She wanted to go home—wherever home was, whatever home meant. She wanted to sleep, to sleep and be alone. "A lesson in love," Massimo had said to the boys. But was this love? Could this brutal, primitive passion be called love? She shook her head wearily. Massimo's love, if he felt love at all, was reserved for others . . . for calm, beautiful, perfectly groomed ladies. His wife. Miriam. Jenny pressed the back of one hand to her damp forehead.

Massimo led her out of the *piazza* just as a man in the gunmetal-gray uniform of the Genoa police entered from another street.

Chapter 4

MASSIMO GRIPPED THE wheel of the car with hands so taut that the veins stood out sharply on their backs.

"That was a foolish thing to do, Jenny," he said when they were halfway home. His voice was calmer now, without the knife-edge of fury it had had in the *piazza*.

Jenny looked out the window of the car. The sun was disappearing from the wide boulevards as it had earlier from the narrow streets of *centro*, and lights were beginning to come on. There was nothing more to be frightened of. Jenny felt more confident with each passing block, but also more contrite.

"Yes," she agreed softly, nestling back against the suede upholstery.

Massimo turned his head abruptly toward her, and the car swerved slightly. "What?" he demanded.

"Yes," Jenny said more firmly. "It was foolish. I didn't stop to think, to see where I was. I'm sorry I caused you trouble. I'm grateful that you followed me."

Massimo nodded with a certain smugness. "All right, then."

"But I was trying to prove a point," Jenny continued thoughtfully. "And the point is a valid one. If I'd had my wits about me, instead of just rushing around, trying to get away from you, I *would* have found my way by myself. Next time I'll keep track of where I'm going."

"Damn it, Jenny!" Massimo exploded. "There will *be* no next time. Not while you're staying with me—not while you're my responsibility!" He lifted one hand from the wheel and slapped it against the dashboard with a resounding crack.

"I am not your responsibility, Massimo," Jenny replied evenly. "I am very much my own responsibility. That's exactly the point. I've had *enough* of other people taking me under their wings."

Heavy traffic, homeward bound at the end of the work day, stopped the car briefly, and Jenny glanced at Massimo. He stared fixedly ahead out the windshield, and his hands clenched and unclenched rhythmically on the steering wheel. The leather-wrapped wheel was damp where his palms rested.

"And I am tired of taking responsibility for other people," he said finally, softly. "But sometimes it is necessary."

Massimo was silent for the remainder of the journey home, and only when he pulled to a stop outside the apartment did he speak again.

"You will excuse me, Jenny, but I must return to my office." He didn't look at her; his eyes stared straight ahead.

"Of course," Jenny answered, surprised. She let herself out, and as she crossed the sidewalk to the apartment entrance, the car moved slowly away, down the street.

Inside, she could hear the muffled sounds of the children playing on the terrace. She hesitated momentarily. A dose of their innocence and vitality would probably feel good.

But she turned down the long corridor toward her room, closing the door behind her. There was no sense in seeing the children more than necessary—in becoming attached to them, or letting them become attached to her. She was more determined now than ever to find her own apartment at the earliest possible moment, and falling in love with the children as well as their father would only make that harder.

Falling in love. Jenny reluctantly turned the phrase over in her mind. It was the first time she had used it about Massimo, and it reverberated strangely. She knew she was attracted to him—more attracted, perhaps, than she had even been to Simon at first. She pulled her slacks and shirt off and lay back on the bed in her underwear, letting the satiny coverlet caress her skin. Falling in love— is that what I'm doing, she asked herself. And a voice inside her head answered: it's what you've already done.

Jenny turned over and buried her face in the soft pillows. *"Sai pazza,"* she said aloud, her words muffled by the pillows. "You really are a crazy lady." Then, with a heavy sigh, she got up and began preparing for her first day of work.

She spent the remainder of the evening rearranging her design portfolio for the hundredth time, poring over a map of bus routes that she had picked up, and selecting clothes to wear—a full, beige wool skirt with deep, slash pockets and a tomato-red silk shirt—for her first day at Gabriella Fortuna's studio. She was in bed by ten and, despite misgivings, slept well and deeply, untroubled by dreams or by memories of the traumatic day.

The next morning, having carefully set her travel alarm for eight o'clock, she was ready to go at nine. Unwilling to confront whoever might be in the dining room, she downed a cup of coffee and nibbled on some toast in the kitchen. She was letting herself out of the apartment when a bright red sports car pulled up to the curb.

Luca unfolded his coltish body from it. His long legs were encased in jeans, and he wore a white shirt with several buttons open. A tweed jacket was slung casually across his shoulders.

"Jenny! *Ciao!* I hoped I would catch you—I will drive you to Gabriella's, *si?*"

He crossed the sidewalk in one stride and grasped Jenny's hand in his.

"Luca! *Buon giorno!*" Jenny felt a smile take over her face. It was impossible not to be cheerful in response to Luca's open good nature. "I was just going to hunt down the number 19 bus stop. It's just down the street..." She gestured with her free hand.

"Oh, no, no, no." Luca shook his head and waggled a finger at her. "Not by bus, not your first day. There will be plenty of time for such things. Today you must arrive by chariot. Come." He took the portfolio away from her and pulled at her hand, leading her across the sidewalk to the little car.

Jenny laughed. "Okay, *si,*" she agreed. "I'd be nervous about missing my stop anyway."

Luca grinned, and his face seemed to glow with genuine pleasure. He was, Jenny thought with a quick shake of her head, irresistible—and an utter contrast to his brother. He must be about her own age—twenty-eight or twenty-nine, certainly—yet there was an enchanting, innocent boyishness about him.

There had been a moment yesterday when she had found Massimo boyish, but that impression had been erased by the sharp brutality, almost viciousness, of his actions at the little *piazza.* Luca's emotions played openly across his face for everyone to see; Massimo's seemed always hidden beneath half-closed eyelids.

Luca opened the door for Jenny with a flourish and helped her into the tiny red car.

He tucked his long legs beneath the steering wheel and pulled away from the curb; his knee rested casually against Jenny's in the cramped space. Luca's driving, unlike his brother's, was adventuresome, accompanied by squealing brakes and shaking fists. Jenny clung to the door handle, grateful that the open car seemed well built.

She heaved a little sigh of relief when they pulled to a halt, ten minutes later, in front of a small, ancient building in the shadows of the ruined opera house. Its only distinctive feature was its door, painted a bright Mediterranean blue. A small, pewter-colored plaque beside the door read simply GABRIELLA FORTUNA.

Luca clambered out of the car and loped around to Jenny's side. He pulled the door open and helped her out, then reached in again to retrieve the portfolio, which he had tucked behind the bucket seats.

"Thank you so much, Luca—*grazie mille.*" Jenny held her hand out, but he kept hold of the portfolio.

"Ah, no, no, no," he said again as he had outside the apartment. "You must not enter the tiger's den alone!" He grinned and took Jenny's elbow, steering her across the wide sidewalk to the blue door.

"Really, Luca, I'm just fine..."

But Luca was already starting up the steps, still clutching her design case in one hand and her elbow in the other.

"Tiger's den," Jenny repeated to herself. She had read that Gabriella was a perfectionist. She worked her designers hard, and she worked hard herself. Her publicity and her letters to Jenny were a little eccentric, true— she clearly had an artist's temperament. But only Luca had implied that she might really be intimidating.

Jenny felt a flash of fear as Luca pushed at the blue door. What if Gabriella Fortuna really *was* a tiger? She had a sudden vision of herself the previous day in the little *piazza* in *centro,* and the doubts she had felt briefly then came flooding back. Had she made some grievous mistake, leaving New York—and Simon—behind, striking out on her own?

The doubts dissolved as Jenny stepped into a large reception room as blue and gay as the front door and was immediately enveloped by a pair of long, thin arms that wrapped her in a hug full of warmth and welcome.

"Signorina Armstrong! Jennifer! *Benvenuto a Genova, e mia casa!"* Gabriella's voice was deep and gravelly, full of years of cigarette smoke, and the grin that split her face almost in two was outlined in bright scarlet lipstick. "We watch for you, dear, and we are all on the needles and pins!"

Gabriella was as tall as Jenny had imagined, almost six feet, and she wore a bright purple tunic over a pair of equally electric yellow knickers. High, red suede boots completed the outfit—one that would have seemed ludicrous on anyone else but that somehow looked exactly right on Gabriella Fortuna.

Jenny found herself returning both the grin and the hug. "I'm so happy to be here," she said, hearing the relief in her own voice. It was going to be all right.

"I am so glad," Gabriella continued effusively. "You had not too bad a trip, eh? You are in comfort with Massimo? Everything is okay, *si?"*

Jenny nodded at the flood of questions. "Yes, yes, everything is just fine, thank you so much."

"And these are Giorgio and Antonio and Stefania..." Gabriella was gesturing vaguely at the little knot of people who were just then entering the room from another door. She added a few more names, and Jenny looked at them, wide-eyed. "These are our designers."

"I'm afraid I'll have to sort out your names," Jenny said, smiling despairingly. They all—four men and two women—smiled back, and one small woman rolled her eyes toward Gabriella.

"Don't worry," she said with a soft laugh. "We will have time."

Gabriella turned to the group. "Now shoo, shoo. I must show Jennifer all over." The small woman dutifully opened the door again, and the six designers filed out of the room.

Then Gabriella turned toward Luca, as if noticing him

for the first time, and her eyes narrowed.

"Luca. *Buon giorno. Come vai?*" Her voice was flat, almost without interest.

"*Bene, bene,* Gabriella." He moved a step closer and planted a kiss on the tall woman's cheek. It was not returned. "*E tua, mia cara?*"

Gabriella shrugged. "I go pretty well, Luca. Pretty well. The spring show was successful, as you know; so now we have many orders to fill. Some things we have problems with." She watched him with her bright green eyes, and the tiny spots of red in his cheeks seemed to darken. Then his smile returned.

"Massimo wanted to come this morning, to bring your new helper," he said. His voice was light and teasing. "But I won our little argument. He said that it had been too long since he had seen you, but I sent him off to work instead."

Luca grinned and winked at Jenny, and Jenny wondered if such an argument had really taken place—if Massimo had wanted to drive her this morning. Somehow it seemed unlikely; from what she had seen of the brothers' relationship, it was hard to believe that Luca *ever* won an argument.

Gabriella nodded gravely. Emotions played on her face as clearly as they did on Luca Silvano's. Jenny could see a tense annoyance darken the green eyes for a moment.

"It *has* been too long," Gabriella said sternly. "You tell him that, Luca. Much too long."

Jenny's mind raced. There was a chiding familiarity in Gabriella's voice. Was it possible that there *was* some kind of understanding between Massimo and Gabriella, just as Luca had hinted at dinner that first night? An engagement, even? Jenny felt a tightening in her stomach. Perhaps it was just as she had imagined then, in her anger; perhaps he toyed with as many women as would have him: Gabriella, the pale, mysterious Miriam; Jenny herself. She set her jaw. All the more reason to step carefully with him.

In any case, Gabriella was clearly annoyed; Massimo had been neglecting her. And that was surely the reason for her shortness with Luca.

Luca pecked Jenny's cheek, handed her the portfolio, and said his good-byes. He was almost out the door, and Gabriella had begun speaking again, when he turned suddenly, a bemused expression on his face.

"Cara Jenny," he said, fixing his eyes directly on hers. "I have done a stupid thing." He smiled like a guilty little boy and patted his jacket pockets with his hands. "I have come out without my wallet. Have you by any chance a few thousand *lire?* I can pay you back this evening." The red spots on his cheeks expanded slightly; he was obviously embarrassed.

"Of course, Luca." Jenny put down the design case and hunted in her purse, pulling out a ten-thousand *lire* note.

Luca took it and, grasping both of Jenny's hands in his, planted a kiss on her mouth. *"Grazie mille,"* he murmured. "You save my life. I pay you back tonight, I promise." And then he turned and was out the door.

Jenny looked back to Gabriella. The tall woman's face was set in a frown, and she was shaking her head slowly. For a brief moment, Massimo's cryptic warning about his brother flashed into Jenny's head: "One must have some care . . . He is not a boy."

Then she shrugged. After all, what was ten thousand *lire* compared to the things Massimo seemed to be asking of her?

"Isn't it always the way?" she said lightly. "The folks with all the money are always forgetting to carry any."

"Eh," Gabriella muttered, dismissing the incident with a wave of her hand. Then her broad smile returned, and the two women set off on a tour of the design studio.

Jenny forced her random thoughts about the brothers Silvano out of her mind, concentrating instead on learning all there was to know about how the House of Fortuna operated.

The rest of the day was busy and confusing—busier and more confusing than any single day Jenny could remember, but more gloriously enjoyable as well. Gabriella could seem eccentric and muddled, but when it came to her business she was a model of efficiency. In New York, Jenny had worked at a large sportswear firm, with almost thirty designers working anonymously. Here there were just the eight of them—the other six designers, Gabriella, and Jenny—and a handful of production and sales workers. They worked as a disciplined team, but each member of the team was a talented and quirky individual.

Gabriella's studio was geared to the two annual shows, spring and fall, in Milan, where the Fortuna collections were shown side by side with those of other top Italian designers. The spring show had taken place a few weeks earlier, and now Gabriella's staff was primarily concerned with making minor adjustments for particular customers and filling orders as quickly as possible. It was a demanding time of year in terms of speed and efficiency, but the extreme tension that preceded a show was temporarily dissolved. The six designers were relaxed and friendly, and they made Jenny feel entirely welcome.

Gabriella and Jenny shared sandwiches and coffee in Gabriella's jumbled office at lunchtime, and the older woman touched on her relationship with the Silvanos.

"My family is very aristocratic," she said with a smile, "but very poor. We are long friends of the Silvanos—generations. There are many marriages between us. *Signora* Silvano likes me especially." A mischievous grin spread across Gabriella's face. "So when I began to design, she provided the money." She took a huge bite of her toasted sandwich and chewed. "I have long since paid that back, but the *Società Silvano* continues to handle all my finances."

She studied the sandwich with a grave expression for a moment. "Sometimes I am tempted to change things, to hire my own business staff here. I am afraid that the Fortuna finances no longer interest the great *Società* very much. Massimo, since he is Director, has expanded it, and now . . . things sometimes seem to . . . slip through the cracks."

Jenny listened curiously. Gabriella's sharp features, really too big for their narrow setting, had a remarkable beauty. Intelligence and good humor shone in her large green eyes, even surrounded as they were by thick mascara and eyeliner. And the designer's English, Jenny noted with amusement, improved no end when she was speaking in private, rather than putting on a public show.

But she wondered what Gabriella meant about things slipping through the cracks. It hadn't taken Jenny long to realize that the Silvano banking group was one of Genoa's major financial institutions. Surely such a large and respected corporation didn't let things slip, no matter how small a part of their business was involved. Was this, she mused, another clue to Massimo's personality? Was he as irresponsible with money as he seemed to be with women? It hardly seemed likely, given his position as Director of the *Società,* but then . . .

It was six o'clock when the designers began packing up and drifting out of the building. An exhausted Jenny accompanied Giorgio down to the sidewalk; the pleasant young designer had promised to point out the number 19 bus stop to her. But once again her experiments with bus routes were not destined to be.

The gray Fiat was parked directly in front of the blue door. Jenny hesitated on the steps of the building.

"Buona sera, Jenny," Massimo called as he pushed the car door open for her. "The children wanted to come

and fetch you home." His expression was polite, non-committal.

Jenny peered into the back seat. Angela's round face smiled back at her, and next to it was Nino's longer, more solemn one.

"Oh, please, Jenny, come with us!" Angela called.

"Well, that's an invitation I can't resist," Jenny responded with a smile. She waved good-bye to Giorgio and climbed in.

Massimo glanced at her briefly. "The children wanted to come," he repeated flatly.

"But *Papà,* it was *your* idea," Nino piped softly from the back seat. Jenny turned her head to look at him and caught a sly smile on his normally sober face. She glanced at Massimo, but he seemed not to have heard. His attention was focused on maneuvering the car into the line of traffic now pouring along the street.

"Did you have a good time? *Zia* Gabriella is wonderful, no?" Angela's high-pitched voice was full of enthusiasm. "I *love zia* Gabriella!"

Jenny turned her head again. "Yes," she agreed, "Gabriella is quite wonderful—you're absolutely right, Angela. I had a wonderful day."

Angela nodded her head smugly, as though she had been quite sure all along that Jenny would feel that way.

"I also had *un giorno meraviglioso*—the very best!" The next few minutes were full of descriptions of school and playtime with friends and with *papà,* and how happy they had been when he had said they would be picking up the *signorina.*

From the corner of her eye, Jenny could see Massimo's sharp profile, his dark eyes flicking continually from the windshield to the rearview mirror, checking traffic. A small smile played at his lips as Angela chattered; his daughter clearly amused him. Jenny saw again in her mind's eye the look of almost painfully pure love that had radiated from father to children when he had first introduced them to her two days ago.

Two days! It seemed like weeks, even months. A lifetime, perhaps. Jenny lost track of what Angela was saying as she watched Massimo. Time enough to feel threatened by this confident man, whose face showed the scars of pain and sorrow. Time enough to fall in love with him. Against all better judgment, there it was. Despite his arrogance, despite his harshness, despite his uncertain relationships with other women. Jenny chewed at her lower lip. It was a fact, not to be denied.

"Jenny? Jenny?" Angela's hand shook her shoulder from the back seat. "Do you think so? Could you, please?"

The question had obviously already been asked more than once, and Jenny had not heard. Massimo glanced at her curiously. She felt a flush of red in her cheeks as his gold-rimmed eyes rested on her face momentarily.

"I'm sorry, Angela, I didn't hear. What were you asking?"

"She asked if you—and I—could eat supper with them on the terrace tonight." Massimo's voice sounded amused. He reached a hand out from the wheel and patted Jenny's knee gently, as though she were a child who needed reassuring. "And I for one would enjoy that very much."

Jenny felt a blaze of heat where his hand touched her leg. "Of . . . of course," she said. "I'd like that, too."

Massimo let his hand rest on her leg for a moment, then took it away. Jenny rubbed absently at the fabric of her skirt where he had touched it; even the material felt heated to her.

The evening was warm, with a gentle, moist, late-May breeze. Back at the apartment, Jenny slipped off her stockings and exchanged her fashionable pumps for light sandals. She pulled the knot out of her hair and shook it loose, abandoning even the tortoiseshell combs. She let the hot water run in the sink until it was steamy,

then soaked a thick washcloth in it and buried her face
in the luxurious warmth, letting it penetrate every pore.
Finally she joined the others on the terrace.

Jenny stretched out on a chaise longue and sipped a
glass of wine, letting her body relax from the long day.
The children chattered on and played rough-and-tumble
games with Massimo while waiting for supper, and Jenny
watched, her pleasure tinged with sadness.

There was a loving casualness in the family's relationships with one another that she envied, that made her
heart quicken a little. Massimo with his children seemed
so open and vulnerable, so eminently trustworthy—so
entirely unlike Simon. Jenny's thoughts ranged back over
the previous day, over the hours he had spent guiding
her with playful intelligence through the city he so obviously loved. There was a stability to Massimo that
Simon lacked, and a gentleness.

Then she abruptly remembered his arrogance, his patronizing warning about his brother, his anger when she
had claimed the right to wander at will in the city—the
brutal harshness of his kiss in the little *piazza*. And she
could feel again the stirrings that his kiss had provoked
in her own body. With a sigh she turned away from the
threesome beside her and looked out over the lights of
Genoa.

It was almost eight o'clock by the time they had finished their supper. Massimo led his children off to bed.
Jenny helped Rosa clear the dishes, then returned to her
chaise. It was dark, and the lights of the city seemed to
reflect the myriad stars hanging low overhead. The sea
was black, endless, mysterious.

Jenny felt content. Work was exciting; Genoa was
beautiful. Tomorrow she would worry about where to
live for the rest of her time here. Tomorrow she would
confront the problem of Massimo Silvano—and her love
for him. She felt a freedom, a release. She was in control.

So complete was Jenny's contentment that she didn't

even hear Massimo's footsteps on the stone terrace. The feel of his lips grazing her hair was a surprise. She sat up abruptly, startled, and caught his chin with the top of her head.

Massimo came around from the back of the chaise, laughing and rubbing his chin. "You have most interesting ways of saying no," he said, amusement coloring his voice and his eyes. "First you run away, and now you try violence."

"I'm sorry, I...You caught me off guard." Jenny laughed, too, to cover the rush of embarrassment she was feeling. "I was just enjoying the perfect evening. But I really need to get to bed early." She started to swing her legs over the edge of the chaise, but Massimo held up a hand. His eyebrows rose, black against his swarthy skin, and even in the night darkness Jenny could see the gleam of gold in his eyes.

"At nine o'clock?" he asked sarcastically, holding his wrist just a few inches from his eyes to read his watch in the darkness. "I think you could spare me a few more minutes, *si?*"

Jenny shrugged and settled back against the chaise with a smile. "Of course. Please join me." She gestured at a second chaise, a few yards away, and Massimo pulled it closer, leaving just a few feet between them. He stretched out his tall frame along the length of it.

His white shirt was open at the neck, and he had rolled the sleeves up; his forearms were strong and sinewy, with a soft down of black hair. His gray pants pulled taut across the tops of his well-muscled thighs.

"So, my *signorina,* you had a good day with Gabriella?"

Jenny nodded eagerly. "It really was. One of the best days I've ever had."

"You had not such wonderful days in New York, then?"

Jenny was silent a moment, then shrugged. "The place

where I worked was bigger and much less personal. Gabriella's is almost like a family. Everyone is nice, and very funny and—"

"And you would like to have a family? You are looking for a family?"

Jenny was vaguely annoyed at his seemingly deliberate misunderstanding. "No, no," she said insistently. "I mean, it's just a much more pleasant work situation. I think I can produce more in this kind of setting. And I'll certainly enjoy it more."

"And after work, when you went home to your husband in New York, you had not a family then either." It was a statement, not a question, as though Massimo had a very clear picture of her life with Simon. She glanced at him sharply, her annoyance growing as he persisted in nudging her into personal revelations. Then she sighed. Why not? It might be a relief to talk.

"I was very much in love with Simon when I first knew him," she said. "He was strong, and I wasn't..." She hesitated.

"My wife was like what you must have been then," Massimo said softly. Jenny turned her head to look at him. It was the first time he had mentioned his wife since he had referred to her death, almost casually, when he and Jenny had first met on the train.

"She was young. She seemed very unsure of herself. But she was very beautiful, and I thought I saw a great vitality in her. I thought I could bring that out, that I could be her teacher, her guide..."

He laughed, and the laughter was harsh. "Well, I succeeded. Beyond my wildest dreams. She discovered passion, and then she decided to find herself other teachers—and finally to become a teacher herself. Of every man who crossed her path. Every man, even..." His words trailed off.

"Did you...Did you love her?" Jenny saw in her mind the cool, lovely face in the living room photo. An emotionless face. She stared at Massimo's profile, outlined now by the lamps at the back of the terrace. His eyelids almost covered his eyes, and what could still be seen of them seemed empty, like black, bottomless wells. His narrow lips curled slightly at the corners, as though he were considering some monstrous joke that had been played on him.

Suddenly he turned his head, and those heavy eyes caught Jenny's and held them in an intense, intimate gaze.

"I loved her, yes." His voice was hoarse with emotion, but whether it was love or hate Jenny couldn't tell. "But she never knew what love was. She knew only pleasure."

Massimo's eyes remained for a long moment on Jenny's face, flickering upward to the thick fringe of hair above her brow, downward to her full lips, then fastening once again on her eyes. Then he let his gaze move slowly down the length of her body, following its contours.

Jenny felt her muscles tighten as his eyes ranged over her, almost as though there were a physical connection between them. It was like a chain reaction: wherever his gaze explored, her nerves and muscles responded as if to a charge of electricity. She clenched her fists. She could not take her eyes from his dark, compelling face.

Had he simply reached over and touched her, Jenny thought later, or even kissed her, she might have resisted. She might have had the strength to push his hand away, or turn her head. But instead he moved off his own chaise and knelt beside her on the terrace, burying his face in the soft wool of her skirt, as a child might. She could feel the warmth of his cheek against her belly through the thin fabric.

And she reacted instinctively. She rested one comforting hand on his thick black hair, stroking it gently and running a finger around the rim of his ear. They remained that way a long moment, almost motionless, with only the small strokes of Jenny's hand breaking the stillness.

Then suddenly Massimo raised himself beside her and slid one hand beneath her skirt, lifting the soft fabric away from her legs and letting his hand rest on the inside of one bare, silken thigh. He watched her face, his eyes dark and serious, waiting for her response as his strong hand caressed the vulnerable flesh.

Jenny felt drawn into those eyes, felt a rising panic as she lost her way in them, drowning...She felt the hardness of his hand against her leg, probing the soft skin, until finally it grazed the wisp of silk that protected her moist, dusky center.

Jenny heard herself moan, and Massimo's eyes, still caught on her own, glowed softly in pleasure. She reached her own hand toward his, pushing at it ineffectually. But his touch only became stronger, and he slid one finger beneath the silk.

Jenny felt a shudder sweep over her body, like an ocean wave washing over her, tumbling her head over heels in warm, dark waters. She remembered wildly once when that had really happened, when she had been a child trapped beneath the ocean's darkness, swimming blindly this way and that, unable to breathe, unable to find her way to the surface.

A blind panic overwhelmed her; she could no longer see Massimo's face, she could only feel his hand exciting her, making her body arch and tighten...The soft, black waters of the ocean were closing over her and bringing with them not death, but some kind of exquisite almost-death.

She reached for Massimo, pulling his body against hers and imprisoning his hand between her legs, needing the feel of it there. Her fingers twined in his hair, and she pulled his face toward hers, opening her mouth to him. He closed his own over it hungrily, pushing hers wide, letting his tongue seek its way inside. Massimo grasped her tangled hair, gathering it in his free hand and wrapping it around his fingers, holding her head motionless against the pillows as his mouth explored hers. They held each other prisoner, feeling each other's needs and meeting them ecstatically. His mouth clung to hers, and then he pulled away, letting that particular bond break in order to form others, elsewhere.

His lips slipped down the column of her throat, and he pressed them to the small, warm triangle at its base, letting his tongue tease at the tiny, wildly irregular pulse that beat there. Jenny's breath quickened, became shallow and fast, and the flesh at the base of her throat burned. There seemed to be some kind of direct connection between that flesh, where Massimo's tongue played, and the hot, moist place between her legs where his fingers still explored, as though a heated wire were stretched between those two small patches of flesh, pulling everything in between taut.

Jenny's hand slid beneath his shirt, exploring the hard muscles of his back and sides. Still he held her head motionless against the pillows of the chaise, his hand wrapped in the mass of her hair. He freed his hand, which had found a welcome between her thighs, and began unbuttoning the bright, fabric-covered buttons of her blouse, slowly at first and then with an increasing urgency, until finally he could pull the tomato-red material aside. His own breath was labored.

Massimo pushed himself up on one elbow and gazed at the creamy flesh of her breasts where they emerged above her bra. One hand stroked them reverently; tenderly, he released first one and then the other from their silken captivity.

"Ah, Jennifer!" His voice was a hoarse whisper; he seemed lost in the beauties of her body. *"Che bella. Tu e bellissima, bellissima . . .* so beautiful . . ."

He lowered his mouth to her breasts, letting the tip

of his tongue glide around them in ever-smaller circles. The flesh at their centers grew dark and hard, and the nipples rose to meet him. He carried her with him, lifting her through the mysterious waters. She arched her breasts toward him. His mouth closed over one, pulling the hard tip of it against his teeth, letting his tongue slip through to play at it. Jenny felt a sharp, exquisite pain as he twisted the nipple in his teeth. The ocean waters were no longer warm but cold, cradling her flesh in their coldness, and she knew she was sinking ever deeper, that she might never again find the surface.

She moved her hands on his back, forcing him against her and feeling his ever-hardening presence at the base of her belly. His mouth teased at her breasts, nipping and pulling at the tender flesh, bringing Jenny to the point of ecstasy and then letting her slip back into mere pleasure. His hand moved down again to the warm triangle below her belly, sliding beneath the silk, reveling in her naked heat, teasing and caressing, and she fought against the ocean waters, trying to find the surface, trying to regain control but not wanting this exquisite suffering to end.

Finally she could wait no longer. She heard her own voice cry out urgently, "Please, Massimo, oh, please . . ."

She shifted her hips against his, feeling his hand push her skirt aside, slide the layers of material downward until there was nothing between them, no barrier, and he was free to come to her, strong and hard, and she found the surface at last, breaking through to the clean, fresh air, and she could breath again, gloriously, wondrously, triumphantly.

Slowly and with great care, Massimo unwound the heavy mass of her hair from around his hand. Jenny was conscious of a tiny line of pain where it had pulled against her scalp, and she blinked, letting her head fall back against the pillows. Massimo's fingers traced her cheek, her mouth, her eyelids.

Jenny drew in a deep breath and let it out slowly, feeling the throbbing in her breasts and between her legs begin to subside.

"Massimo," she began, "I—"

His finger touched her lips. "Shhh. I know."

He leaned back, away from her, supporting himself on one elbow. His eyes were hooded, gleaming pools of darkness in the night.

"You are full of life, *cara mia,*" he murmured. "You need no lessons from me."

Jenny smiled at him tentatively. "But it's never been like this for me, not before," she whispered. "Massimo, I love you."

She touched his arm, but Massimo was strangely silent. She thought suddenly of his other women: the cool, beautiful wife who had abandoned him; Gabriella, with her independent, willful self-confidence; the pale, unknown Miriam. Jenny searched his face for a clue about what he was feeling, but it was hidden in shadows.

"Come, *tesora mia,* my lovely treasure. It's late. Tomorrow we shall talk." His voice was deep and coaxing; it wrapped her in warmth like a cocoon.

She let him replace her clothing, fuss with her blouse and skirt until they looked as though they had never been touched, and pull her upright on the chaise. She felt satiated with pleasure, drunk with it; Simon had never brought her this far. Massimo had carried her with him, waited until she cried out in her need for him.

Does it even matter if he loves me, she wondered, if he can make me feel like this? She smiled at him as he led her from the terrace, a smile of satisfaction and pleasure.

At the door of her bedroom, Massimo kissed her once, gently, on her lips, letting his mouth linger there for only a moment.

"We shall talk tomorrow," he said again. "Sleep well, *tesora mia.*"

Jenny nodded. And sleep, when it came, was full of dreams of sailboats and tall men in white trunks and the hot sun glistening on Mediterranean waves.

Chapter 5

THE ALARM RANG at eight o'clock. Catlike, Jenny stretched her body against the soft sheets before pushing the coverlet aside and sliding her feet over the edge of the bed. Her flesh still remembered Massimo's touch.

She pulled one shutter back from the window for a quick look at the weather and frowned at the thin gray clouds that covered the sky. It looked cool and damp; there was no sign of the lemon-colored sun that had dominated her dreams. But nothing, she thought cheerfully, could interfere with her good humor today. Jenny padded back to the wardrobe and pulled out a pair of slacks—gray flannel to match the sky—and a cranberry-colored cotton sweater. Catching her hair in a silver clip at the nape of her neck, she slipped her feet into tall leather boots and, after one more peek out the window, closed the shutter, pulled her raincoat out of the wardrobe, and slung it over one arm.

The apartment outside her room was silent, and Jenny hummed to herself as she made her way down the long corridor toward the dining room. She would find Massimo there, she was sure, and she was eager to see his face, to watch the play of intelligence across it, to have him smile at her...

As she started through the little entrance foyer, a phone on the table there began to ring. Impulsively, Jenny picked it up.

"Pronto?" She felt a tiny surge of pleasure that she had remembered the proper greeting from her brief Italian classes.

There was a moment of silence. Then a woman's voice spoke, high, childlike and slightly mechanical, like a very expensive music box. The woman wanted Massimo.

"Uno momento," Jenny began. But before she could even cover the receiver to call Massimo, his deep voice came over the line from another extension.

"Jenny," he said, "get off the phone." It was not a request; it was an order. And his tone was hard, like steel.

Jenny blinked. "I'm sorry, Massimo—it was ringing as I walked by, and I picked it up—"

"Get off, Jenny," he interrupted. Then, almost as an afterthought, he added, "Please."

"Massimo," the silvery voice at the other end of the line broke in, *"chi e la? Chi e?"*

"E nessuno, Miriam. Niente," he replied sharply. Then, "Jenny..."

Slowly Jenny replaced the receiver in its cradle. Her hand trembled slightly, and she felt a vague dizziness just behind her eyes.

"Who is there?" the woman had asked. "Who is it?" And Massimo had replied, "It's no one. Nothing." And the woman was Miriam.

Jenny met her own eyes in the mirror over the phone. She stared without comprehension at her face with its full red mouth and pink cheeks, its thick black lashes and frame of heavy reddish hair. It was a face that seemed suddenly *too* full of life. In her mind's eye she saw another face, a small, perfect oval outlined by pale blond hair pulled back into a neat chignon. The eyes were gray, and everything about the face was cool and controlled—everything except those eyes. They were full of love—a painful, overwhelming, intimate love.

How could she have forgotten about Miriam? How could she have thought that last night meant anything to Massimo—anything more than one more conquest? She repeated his words dully to herself: It's no one, nothing.

Jenny turned abruptly away from the mirror and walked slowly into the living room. She paused in front of the piano and sought out the picture of that other face, tucked toward the back among the photographs. She read the inscription again. "With great love, your Miriam."

And he belongs to you, too, Jenny thought blankly. He is yours. How could I have thought, even for a moment, that he might be mine?

Footsteps entered the room behind her, and she whirled to face Massimo, a fierce energy replacing the blankness. The smile he wore was polite and preoccupied rather than tender.

"Ah, Jenny, *ciao*. I wish to apologize for my manner on the phone. I'm afraid you startled me, answering it, and it was a...a private matter." He shrugged.

Jenny raised her eyebrows. "Oh?" she answered sharply. "Private. I see. Of course."

The curtains dropped suddenly over Massimo's eyes; they were dark and impenetrable. "I am afraid I must be away today," he said. "I must go back to Milano, in fact. Some unfinished business."

Jenny stared at him steadily, hoping that her eyes conveyed the icy disinterest she wished she felt.

"Well, of course," she said finally. "Perhaps I'll run into you this evening then."

Massimo shook his head quickly, and Jenny was uncomfortably conscious of his straight, carefully combed black hair following the elegant lines of his head. "I fear not," he said. "Probably my business will keep me away overnight."

"I see," Jenny said again, a tight smile on her lips. She glanced pointedly at her watch. "Well, if I'm going to experiment with the bus today, I'd better be on my way." She looked up at Massimo brightly. "Have a good day in Milan, Massimo. And watch out for lost ladies in train stations. You don't really have room in your life for another one."

Something flashed through Massimo's eyes so quickly that Jenny couldn't identify it. Confusion, perhaps, or even a momentary pain. He took a step forward and raised his hands to her shoulders. Jenny felt her flesh tighten at his touch, and a tiny shudder passed through her body, but she kept her own hands close to her sides. Then he leaned toward her, clearly seeking a kiss. Jenny turned so his lips just brushed her cheek, and their touch felt like a slap on her warm flesh.

Massimo's hands dropped abruptly to his sides. The dark brown centers of his eyes had gone black, and the gold in them shone cold and hard through thick lashes. Then he turned and left the room.

Jenny found the number 19 bus without any trouble. There was a heavy moisture in the air, as if the sea were being pulled up into the atmosphere and somehow held there; it turned the waves of her hair into tight curls. The pleasure she had felt earlier had drained away, and now there was only an emptiness inside her, as though nothing really mattered, as though the sensations of last night had happened to someone else, in some other world.

She pushed the damp mass of her hair behind her ears and fixed the silver clip more firmly into place. It was Simon all over again, that was the infuriating thing. And all she had proved by her little adventure with Massimo was that she was still vulnerable to that kind of male arrogance. Well, no more, she vowed angrily. She clenched one fist and struck it almost unconsciously against her thigh.

Suddenly she noticed that the stout, elderly man sitting opposite was staring at her. She glared back. One of his hands rested on a heavy black cane, and the folds of his chins seemed to melt into his thick stomach. The man pulled the corners of his mouth down into a pout, then pulled them back up into a grin. He pointed at her frown and shook his head, then waggled a finger at his own grin and nodded rapidly.

Jenny felt a twinge of amusement. She must have looked quite a sight, glaring and pounding at herself like that! She let her face relax into a smile, and the man instantly looked so pleased that she laughed in spite of herself. He laughed, too, a hearty chuckle. The other morning commuters around them studied their newspapers intently.

As the bus pulled up in front of the ruined opera house around the corner from Gabriella's studio and Jenny rose to get off, the old man put one finger beside his nose and gave her a huge wink. Charm, Jenny wryly acknowledged, must simply be born into every Italian male.

Jenny felt better. She pushed open the bright blue door to the studio. The first thing to do, obviously, was to renew the hunt for another apartment. Gabriella had said she couldn't find anything, but maybe her efforts had been cut short by the offer from Luca Silvano. Gabriella's help could be enlisted again—right now, today.

But Gabriella was nowhere to be seen. Jenny made her way upstairs to the work room and began going through the fabric samples that Gabriella had accumulated for the fall show, all the while keeping one eye on the office door in hopes that her employer would put in an appearance. But the door remained closed.

At lunchtime Jenny hurried through a toasted sandwich and a *frulate*—a sweet blended drink of milk and fruit—and then visited the several real estate agencies located near the studio. The message at each was the same, however, transmitted clearly despite her minimal Italian and the agents' minimal English: there were no apartments to be had in this Riviera city at this time of year. Perhaps in the fall . . .

Jenny returned to the studio tired and frustrated to find the design room in a state of suspended animation. The other designers were all there, standing by their work-tables staring at one another, some with pencils upraised as if interrupted in midstroke. From the little office came the sounds of half an argument—Gabriella, on the phone, shouting angrily.

Suddenly the office door burst open and Gabriella herself exploded into the work room. Her expressive face was full of fury, and her scarlet-nailed hands sliced through the air like weapons. In one of them she held a letter, and she strode from one designer to the next, waving it beneath their noses. Her husky voice worked rapid-fire like a machine gun, but the Italian came much too fast for Jenny to understand.

Jenny watched and listened in bewilderment. Clearly Gabriella was furious, and it seemed to have something to do with some fabric that hadn't been delivered. But beyond that, Jenny had no notion of what it was all about.

Then suddenly the tone of Gabriella's voice changed. It lowered, and she spoke more slowly. Her great, green eyes glittered like emeralds.

"*E stupido, questo* Silvano," she muttered. "*Irresponsible. Ma non piu, e basta, cosa!*"

Then, as if suddenly settling on a decision she had been considering for some time, she gestured at Giorgio to accompany her and marched back to the office. Just as she reached it, Jenny heard her growl, "*Telefono la mamma. Si.*" She nodded her head once sharply, then slammed the door shut behind herself.

Jenny stared for a moment at the closed door. She had understood almost all of the last speech, but she still didn't know what it meant. Obviously Massimo had done something terrible—something that had made Gabriella angry enough to call him stupid and irresponsible. "No more," she had said, "enough of this!" What on earth could he have done? And had she really heard those last words correctly: "I am calling mamma." Whose mamma? How could someone's *mother* be involved in all this?

Of the other designers, only Giorgio spoke fluent English. And he was closeted with Gabriella in the office. Hesitantly, Jenny turned to plump, dark-haired Stefania.

"Che cosa?" she asked. "What's going on?"

"Eh." Stefania shrugged one shoulder eloquently, implying that the whole thing was much too complicated for any of them to understand completely. "There is trouble over the fabric for the fall. Gabriella, she order *trenta*—is thirty—bolts from a man in Como, make wonderful cloth, but he tell her no, the bill, he is not paid from the last time, for spring. The cloth, he is *necessario*—?" Stefania knit her brow and looked to Jenny for help.

"It's the same in English, necessary," Jenny said quickly. "The fabric is necessary. But what about the Silvanos? Why is she mad at them?"

Stefania nodded impatiently. "Gabriella, she is disgusted. The Silvanos, they pay our bills, they are big money people, *si?* You understand? But often they do not pay on time. This happens before. Gabriella, she say she is up to the top with this. You say, how, the last piece of straw?"

Jenny nodded. "The last straw. The straw that broke the camel's back. You mean this happens regularly?"

"The straw that broke the camel's back," Stefania repeated, pleased with her new phrase. "Why a camel?"

Jenny spread her hands in frustration. "I don't know, Stefania, it's just a saying. But does this kind of thing happen often?"

Stefania shrugged. "Is a big company, *la Società.*

Maybe is better we do our own money. Gabriella, she is unhappy a little for months now."

"But that's just it," Jenny argued more to herself than to Stefania, "it *is* a big company. Surely a banking house or whatever the *Società* is doesn't get big without being responsible. Surely it doesn't make this kind of blunder regularly."

Stefania narrowed her eyes and studied Jenny intently. "Blunder," she said slowly.

"Mistake," Jenny responded, vaguely impatient. "Mistake!"

"Non lo so." Stefania moved back toward her own worktable. "I don't know. Only I know that Gabriella is unhappy with the Silvanos. Only I know that."

Jenny nodded slowly and turned back to the sketches she had begun that morning. She picked up her pencil, and her hand moved mechanically over the first drawing, adding a line here, straightening one there. But what she saw was not the pencil sketch of a dress; it was the outline of a face—Massimo's face, with its sharp lines and hooded eyes. An artist's dream, she thought ironically. Idly, she drew a quick portrait in one corner of the paper; then, feeling a wave of sudden fury at herself and at the situation she had managed to get herself into, she ripped the sheet off her pad and crumpled it in her hand. It was just like him—as it had been just like Simon—to rely on the strength of his charm! He knew, at least with women, that he could repair whatever damage he created, so he didn't much care what the damage was. It was so irresponsible, so calculated, so . . . arrogant!

Jenny's jaw tightened, and she opened her clenched fist, letting the crushed paper fall into the huge wastebasket next to her table. This time he had gone too far. Whatever he had done to Gabriella had been too much— and Jenny had had enough as well. If he could make love to her and then run off to his mistress not twelve hours later . . . Well. There would be no more damage inflicted on *this* lady. No more!

At six o'clock Jenny wearily packed away her pencils and tucked the fabric samples she had been studying into a drawer. On the steps outside the blue door she hesitated for a moment. Gabriella had reappeared once or twice during the afternoon, looking grim, and Jenny hadn't spoken to her. But perhaps now she would be calm enough to give some advice about apartments. Jenny had no doubt that Gabriella would be sympathetic to her desire to get away from the Silvanos.

Resolutely, Jenny turned back toward the door. Her hand was on the handle when she noticed Luca's red Porsche dodging through traffic a little way down the block. It wasn't true, she thought to herself suddenly, that she wanted to get away from *all* the Silvanos. She waved at Luca as the car approached, and he caught her eye.

"Jenny! *Ciao!*" he called, swinging the open car into a parking spot near the curb. He stepped out and covered the distance between them in two strides. His eyes swept approvingly up and down her body as he came closer, and Jenny returned his gaze with amusement. He wore jeans, a white shirt with the buttons left open halfway down his chest, and an expensive-looking herringbone jacket.

"I was afraid I'd miss you!" he said, draping one arm around her shoulders and planting a kiss on her cheek. "The traffic . . . eh!" He made a quick gesture of annoyance and rolled his eyes.

"Why didn't you call if you wanted me to wait for you?" Jenny asked.

Luca looked at the ground almost shyly. "I was afraid if you knew I wanted to take you to dinner, you'd say no. Because you were tired . . . or maybe because I hadn't paid back the money I owe you." He glanced up at her again.

Suddenly Jenny felt lighthearted. She swung her own

arm around Luca's waist and caught her thumb in a belt loop.

"Luca," she laughed, "you're exactly what I need. Let's get some dinner."

Luca grinned at her delightedly, then steered her across the sidewalk toward the car.

He took them first to a large, noisy, smoke-filled *caffè*-bar in *centro,* its walls covered with art deco mirrors and its tables filled with aggressively attractive young Genovese. Luca stopped again and again to acknowledge greetings as he guided her to a table near the back, and Jenny had to admit that being an object of obvious envy to every woman in the place brought a certain satisfaction.

Luca seated Jenny at an empty table and fetched a bottle of white wine for her and a glass of Scotch for himself, then hovered fussily over her for another moment until he had satisfied himself that she was completely comfortable. Jenny felt nicely pampered and somehow lazy; it was not a feeling she had had with Massimo. With Massimo, there was a constant tension, as though she must be always alert, always awake to his challenge.

"Now," Luca said finally, "tell me why you looked so unhappy when I first saw you outside Gabriella's."

"Unhappy?" Jenny asked innocently.

But Luca waggled a finger at her and tilted his head to one side. "Come on, Jenny. Don't try to fool little brother Luca. What is bothering you?"

Jenny sipped her wine and studied the open face before her. Luca's floppy black hair hung charmingly over his forehead, and his dark eyes seemed almost transparent. He had stretched one arm along the back of the banquette seat they shared, and she could feel the light touch of his fingers where they just rested at her back. She felt a sudden, almost irresistible urge to tell him everything—from her dream on the train right through this morning, including Massimo's deserting her for Miriam. It would be nice to have someone to talk to.

"Oh, Luca," she began. "It's Massimo."

But as soon as she had said his name, Jenny had second thoughts. She looked away from Luca's curious gaze, glancing around at the mirrored bar. Her face confronted her from every wall. Luca's arm slid off the banquette and onto her shoulders, and he nodded.

"*Si*. I thought that might be the problem." The look on his face suggested that he was used to dealing with problems his brother had created.

"Oh, it's not that," Jenny said hastily, "not really a *problem*. It's just that . . . Well, he's been kind of attentive, and I have so much to do, getting used to a new place and a new job and all that . . ." Jenny made a vague gesture of confusion as her voice trailed off.

Luca's fingertips began gently massaging the back of her neck, and Jenny could feel her tension melt away at his touch. There was no electricity about the connection between them; she felt no threat. There was only a softness that was lulling, almost hypnotic.

"Tell me," he said gently.

Jenny took a deep breath. She felt divided between two paths. Massimo had given her something beautiful last night, something she had never known existed before. And she had admitted—to herself and to him—that she loved him. She felt a certain loyalty to him, despite what he had done to her this morning. And yet there was a strange compulsion coming to her from Luca, urging her to tell him everything.

"I guess," she said slowly, "it's that I've just barely gotten out of a relationship with one very domineering man—that's why I'm here, in Genoa—and now suddenly there's this other strong presence in my life. It just makes me uneasy."

Luca nodded sympathetically. "Massimo is a very strong man," he agreed with a rueful smile. "I know. I have lived with him all my life. But," he shrugged, "Massimo has many interests."

Jenny jerked her head up to look at him. He seemed to be confirming her worst suspicions.

"If you just pay him no mind," he went on, "Massimo won't bother you for long."

Jenny looked down at the table and picked nervously at her napkin with one finger.

"Oh, Jenny! *Cara mia!*" Luca's voice was almost a lament. "You *want* my brother to bother you!" She felt him looking at her, and finally she raised her head and met his gaze, nodding almost imperceptibly.

Immediately, she regretted it. "I don't know what I want, Luca," she said, shaking her head.

"Ah, Jenny, whatever shall we do with you?" He shook his head, then pulled her close and kissed her on the cheek. "Whatever shall we do? And I had thought there might be hope for myself!" He slid his arm off her shoulders and laid both hands on the table, palms up. It was a gesture that reminded Jenny of Massimo, and she swallowed hard.

"Here is what we shall do," Luca finally said firmly, still grinning. "First we shall have another drink. Then we shall have a delicious dinner. We shall not talk about Massimo for one more second; we shall talk only about things that make us happy. And then, tomorrow, we shall find for you another apartment. *Si?*"

The wine was making a warm space inside Jenny, and Luca's good humor was infectious. The round patches of red at his cheekbones made him look like a cherub, or perhaps some kind of full-grown elf. Jenny giggled and nodded.

"That sounds terrific, Luca." She raised her glass in a toast to him, and he refilled it from the bottle on their table.

They finished the wine, then made their way slowly out of the bar. In the car on the way to the restaurant

Luca had picked out for dinner, they sang old Broadway show tunes at the top of their voices. Luca knew the words to everything. They didn't mention Massimo again until halfway through the broiled *scampi* that Luca had ordered.

The *scampi* reminded Jenny that she had hardly eaten any lunch, and that she had skipped breakfast altogether in her haste to get out of the apartment that morning. Now her head felt slightly loose, as though it weren't quite properly connected to the rest of her, and she had to lean forward and concentrate hard to hear what Luca was saying. This place was less crowded than the last, but the noise seemed somehow more deafening.

Jenny found herself telling Luca about what had happened at work. "It was kind of funny, when you think about it," she said with a rising giggle. "Gabriella just stomped around the place, waving those incredible fingernails of hers, ranting and raving! Of course, I couldn't really understand what was going on." Jenny put a hand to her mouth and leaned toward Luca. "But if you want to know the truth, she called you dear brother '*stupido*'!"

Luca rested his chin in his palms, his face just a few inches from Jenny's.

"Massimo?" he asked incredulously. "That person we are not to speak about? That person whose attachment to Gabriella, well . . . perhaps we should not speak about that either. She called *him* stupid?"

Jenny nodded. She couldn't understand why the whole episode seemed so amusing to her now. She suppressed a laugh and lowered her voice as though she were imparting a secret. "There were some bills that didn't get paid on time apparently, and she was really angry. And she called him stupid! The great Massimo Silvano!"

Luca gazed at her steadily, his fingers drumming on the table, and the little red patches in his cheeks darkened.

"Why, your eyes can do the same thing Massimo's can!" Jenny blurted suddenly. "They just get blank all

over, like you've drawn the shades! It's really remarkable—" She blinked rapidly several times. "I can't make
mine do that."

Luca glanced quickly away, and when he looked back
at Jenny his eyes were amused again.

"Tell me what Gabriella said," he asked casually.

"Oh..." Jenny shrugged. "I don't know, Luca. I really
couldn't understand. It was all in Italian!" It seemed very
comic that Gabriella had been shouting in Italian, and
Jenny finally began to laugh out loud. Luca laughed with
her, and he reached one hand to her cheek and let it trail
lightly down the line of her jaw. Jenny grinned at him.

"Try to remember," he said. Jenny hardly noticed the
hint of insistence in his voice.

She knit her brow, concentrating furiously on the scene
with Gabriella. "Let's see. Stefania said it was something
to do with a fabric manufacturer who wouldn't send any
more fabric because his last bill hadn't been paid, and
Gabriella was saying that she had had enough and she
wouldn't take anymore..."

Suddenly Jenny's face lit up, and she snapped her
fingers in delight. "And she said something about tele-
phoning somebody's mother! That seemed particularly
strange."

"Somebody's mother?" Luca repeated slowly.

Jenny nodded eagerly, then frowned again. "Who on
earth is *mamma*, Luca? Whose *mamma*?"

Luca leaned back against the plush seat and shrugged
his shoulders. "Sometimes I wonder about Massimo,"
he said with a shake of his head. "He lets things go..."
He was silent a moment, then took a sip of his coffee
and looked at his watch.

"So," he said with a smile, "it was a good dinner,
si?"

"Oh, wonderful, Luca—thank you!" Jenny agreed.
"Especially since I haven't eaten all day."

"And this maybe excuses my debt to you?" he asked

softly, looking down at the table.

"Oh, of course, Luca. Don't worry about it."

"Now," he went on, "let's talk of other things." He leaned forward again and touched her cheek. "I am told Massimo is in Milano for the night."

Jenny nodded, but she felt a twist at the pit of her stomach. "So he told me," she said dryly.

"Perhaps you would like to go back to the apartment and have a glass of wine?" Luca was looking at her with his wide, round eyes; his whole face glowed in the soft light. His fingers traced little circles on her cheek. He *was* attractive, Jenny told herself, returning his gaze, and yet she couldn't suppress a tiny giggle. His charm, de-lightful as it was, seemed so casually calculated after Massimo's unpredictable sharp edges.

"I bet you get just about everything you want," she said with a laugh.

Luca continued to look at her, a small smile tilting his lips. "Just about," he agreed. "Let's go home."

The air had cleared during the day, and the stars hung low over the city as Luca guided the little sports car up the hill to the Silvano apartment. He pulled the car to the curb in front of the building and turned in the seat to face Jenny.

"Cara mia," he said softly. "You are so beautiful."

Jenny smiled broadly. "How nice of you to say so!" She reached over and patted his knee. "And you're ter-ribly good-looking yourself." She leaned back against the seat with a sigh. "And so rich! I've never known so many rich people before!"

She shook her head sharply and giggled. "I can't be-lieve I said that," she whispered in a conspiratorial tone. "It's not like me!"

Luca's hand rested on Jenny's knee now, and he leaned toward her. "But it's true, little one. I can make you happy."

Jenny looked at him. "Why couldn't I have fallen in

love with *you?*" she asked, laughing. "You're so uncomplicated!"

"Would it be so hard?" he asked softly. "To fall in
love with me?" His hand was making little stroking motions on her leg, and it felt warm and comfortable. Jenny
batted it away good-naturedly.

"Oh, Luca, I can't be in love with two people at once!
Tell you what." She looked at him, but his face seemed
unfocused. It was the bright glitter of the stars, she told
herself, making it impossible for her to see. She waved
her hand vaguely in front of her face, trying to clear her
vision. "Tell you what. As soon as I get over your brother,
I'll put you next on my list! Definitely." Then she leaned
back against the seat and let laughter overtake her completely.

She was still shaking with amusement when they entered the apartment, supporting one another with inter-
twined arms, and that was why she didn't immediately
see the tall figure standing in the archway that led into
the living room.

"Buona sera." Massimo's voice cut through the air
like a knife, quiet but slightly hoarse, as though he were
keeping it quiet by some vast effort of will. "Something
is funny?"

"Good evening, Massimo," Luca said, moving slightly
away from Jenny but keeping one hand under her elbow.
"I understood you were spending the night in Milano."

Massimo's face was absolutely still, as if carved from
brittle stone. "Get out of here, Luca."

Jenny's laughter trailed off into a tiny burp.

"Get out!" Massimo said again, and this time his voice
was louder, less hoarse. There was a hint of contained
violence in it as there had been at the little *piazza* in
centro.

Luca, his mouth turned up in an ironic smile, bowed
first toward his brother and then, more deeply, toward
Jenny. Without another word, he turned and stepped back

out the still-open door and disappeared. Jenny, without Luca's hand on her arm, felt a shuddery weakness; she rested one hand on the little table to support her suddenly rubbery legs.

"We had dinner," she said, smiling rather vacantly at Massimo.

He stared for a moment longer at the door through which Luca had left, then moved abruptly across the foyer and slammed it shut. He turned to face Jenny. "You're drunk," he said. His voice and his body seemed all hard edges.

Jenny shook her head fiercely. "I'm *never* drunk," she responded, feeling defiance replace amusement deep inside her. But suddenly she knew he was right; she *had* drunk too much, on an almost empty stomach. How else to explain some of the things she had said to Luca? And now she could hardly stand up! She put both hands down carefully on the table and straightened her shoulders, taking a slow, deep breath. Her head cleared a little. She looked at Massimo in the shadowy light, and as she did, a wave of anger overtook her.

"Besides," she said, furious, "what business is it of yours? *You* weren't here; *you* were off in Milan." The anger became rage as she spoke. "What I do with my time has nothing to do with you. You don't own me, Massimo!"

Massimo took half a step forward, then stopped himself. He folded his arms across his chest, as if holding in the strength of his body.

"Milan was something I had to do, Jenny. You did not have to get drunk with my brother."

Jenny stared at him, at his dark face and hooded eyes, which were glittering like coal in the shadows. "Has it occurred to you that maybe I *enjoy* being with Luca?" she said harshly. Then she pulled her hands from the table and turned abruptly down the corridor, slamming the door of her bedroom behind her.

Chapter 6

JENNY STOOD IN her darkened room, fists clenched at her sides and her head suddenly remarkably clear. She saw the two brothers in her mind's eye. If only she had met *Luca* first, if only it had been he rather that Massimo on that train. But even as the thought raced through her head, she knew it wouldn't have worked. It was Massimo she loved, not Luca. And part of what she loved about him was his hardness, the unexpectedness of his tender compassion, his strength...

She kicked her boots off with a ferocious gesture and shrugged her raincoat off her shoulders, letting it slip to the floor.

Suddenly the door flew open, and Massimo strode into the room. He snapped on the overhead light, flooding everything with a brightness that hurt Jenny's eyes. She whirled to face him.

"What do you think you're doing?" she asked, her voice carefully under control.

"I told you last night that we would talk today," he said. "It is still today. So now we talk."

The control shattered. "How dare you?" Jenny exploded. "How dare you march into my room as if..."

"As if I owned it? I do."

Jenny glared at him. She could feel the heat rising through her body, darkening her cheeks from pink to scarlet. Every nerve felt stretched to its absolute limit.

"So you do," she said through clenched teeth. "And I hope I won't have to impose on your hospitality very much longer."

Massimo watched her, his face sharply outlined by the bright ceiling light and his arms once again folded across his chest. He made a quick gesture of dismissal with one hand.

"Of course you will stay," he said. "That is not the issue. The issue is what kind of games you are playing."

Jenny's mouth fell open. "Games? *Me?* I hardly think you have the right to accuse *me* of playing games!" Her voice sounded unnaturally loud, almost wild, to her ear.

Massimo's eyes were steady and blank, wells of pure darkness. "You make love to me and then to my brother," he said grimly. "I call that playing games."

Jenny stepped backward instantly, as though she had been struck. She raised one hand to her fiery cheek. For a brief moment, she wanted to defend herself, to try to explain why she had been with Luca, to ask for Massimo's forgiveness—as she would have done during those first years with Simon. Then fury won out.

"Get out," she said quietly. "Right now."

Massimo moved half a step toward Jenny, as he had done in the hall, and then stopped. His arms remained folded, and his lips were pressed tightly together. For a long moment he was absolutely still, and then his face suddenly seemed to collapse. The hardness of it fell abruptly away, and something that Jenny could only identify as pain filled his eyes. She lifted one arm toward him just as he turned away and left the room, shutting the door carefully behind himself.

Jenny stared blindly at the closed door. Two images hung in the air before her: his back as he had turned away from her, the tailored jacket outlining his wide shoulders, the even line of his black hair where it just brushed the top of his shirt collar; and his face suddenly without defenses, open and vulnerable, full of pain.

She took two steps forward and switched off the light, then turned back to the bed. Coldness seemed to envelop her as she stretched out on it, so she pulled the coverlet around her like a cocoon. It felt warm and smooth against her now-icy cheeks—the same cheeks that had been full of fire only moments earlier.

What have I done, she asked herself dismally. Why do things always have to be so complicated? She felt small tears forming at the corners of her eyes, and she wiped at them angrily. He had no right . . .

Suddenly she pushed the coverlet aside and sat up, swinging her long legs over the side of the bed. The symptoms were laughably familiar; a man making her feel that she had somehow failed him, making her crawl into bed to wonder where *she* had gone wrong, when in fact it was he who had betrayed her. It was Massimo, after all, who had run off to Milan only hours after making love to her.

Jenny planted her bare feet firmly on the carpet and pushed herself up, straightening her shoulders with a vigorous shake. She was the one with the right to be angry, and he owed her an explanation. Besides, she thought, her resolve softening a little, he had looked so unhappy.

She took a deep breath and blew it out slowly, feeling a sense of calm invade her body. Then, stepping out into the corridor, she closed the door gently behind her.

Jenny wasn't sure which room was Massimo's. But only one door, at the far end of the hall, showed light beneath it. She knocked quietly, unwilling to risk waking the children who were asleep back down the hallway.

Massimo's voice responded immediately. *"Si? Che cosa?"*

"It's me, Massimo," she said firmly. "May I come in?"

There was a moment of silence before he answered. "Yes, of course."

Jenny pushed open the door.

Massimo's room was on the opposite side of the corridor from her own, and his window faced out over the city of Genoa. The inside shutters were flung wide, and the window itself was open to the night air. The room seemed warm and moist and full of moonlight. The light Jenny had seen under the door came from a small lamp on a desk near the door.

Massimo was standing in front of the window. He had started to undress—his shirt and jacket lay in a crumpled pile on a chair, and his feet were bare. Brown slacks with small pleats at the waist covered the lower half of his body, but they fitted so smoothly over his narrow hips and legs that they served only to emphasize the rest of his nakedness. The moon, shining brilliantly through the window, outlined Massimo's body with a delicate, silvery light.

Jenny sucked in her breath. *This* seemed hardly fair. Last night, in the darkness on the terrace, she had taken a giddy pleasure in touching that smooth, hard chest; now her eyes drank in the coppery skin, the rippling planes and muscles. She felt a rising dizziness, and she knew that if she continued to stare at him, she would end by reaching toward him and stroking the taut flesh, touching his carved cheek...

She looked at his face for a moment. It was impassive, all pain erased, and the eyes were sober and chestnut colored. One eyebrow was slightly raised, curious.

Jenny tore her eyes away with an effort of will and looked around the room. It was lovely, more stark and modern than her own, but with touches that surprised her: an exquisite American quilt hung on one wall, a framed poster of an exhibit of Etruscan pottery on another. Above the desk by the door hung two small paintings in perfect jewellike colors, identifiable even to Jenny's amateur eye as medieval.

The wall-to-wall carpeting was slate-blue, and the big wooden bedstead was covered by an African-looking weaving in lovely earth tones. Photos of the children sat on a bookcase next to the bed, and the bookcase itself held a variety of titles—mysteries, classics in English, some heavy-looking texts on international banking. Jane Austen's *Pride and Prejudice* lay on a small wooden trunk at the end of the bed.

Jenny had pictured Massimo in a room surrounded by elegant antiques, dark wood, and perhaps the trappings of his coolly beautiful former wife. This room surprised her.

She looked back at Massimo, who stood exactly as he had when she had entered the room. One hand rested on the wide windowsill and the other hung loose at his side. His hair, usually perfectly groomed, was slightly tousled, as though he had recently run a hand through it. But his face, which had been emotionless when she opened the door, now held a small, wry smile.

"Do you approve?" he asked. "Does my room pass inspection?" He slid his hips up onto the broad sill and sat facing her, his back to the moonlight and his bare feet dangling just above the rug.

Jenny blew a little puff of air upward. Her cheeks were beginning to feel warm again, and she was very close to regretting the burst of independence that had prompted this impulsive move.

"It's . . . it's a lovely room, Massimo. Of course." Her words sounded very prim. "But I didn't come to inspect it. Or you."

Massimo's black eyebrows rose, and he gave a tiny, amused nod in her direction. Jenny kept her eyes determinedly on his face, refusing to let them fall to his chest with its hint of black hair set against the coppery smoothness.

"Oh," he said, forcing a seriousness back onto his face. "Then what did you come for?"

"I felt you were very unfair just now," Jenny began quickly. "What you said about me and Luca..." Her voice rose slightly, and she stopped and swallowed hard, willing it back under control. If only he would put a shirt on!

Massimo rested his strong hands on the broad sill on either side of him. "Yes?" he asked. "How was that?"

Strange things were happening in Jenny's stomach, and the vague feeling of dizziness kept coming and going in waves. It was not the same kind of dizziness she had felt earlier, from too much wine... Massimo's bare, dark torso gleamed in the moonlight, and she was uncomfortably conscious of his toes just grazing the thick blue rug as he swung them lightly. She lowered her gaze to the carpet and began studying it intently.

"Well," she said finally, clearing her throat of an unexpected hoarseness, "I wanted you to know that you had no right to accuse me of... of anything improper with Luca. We had dinner together, that's all, and I resent the implication that I led either one of you on."

She dug the toes of one foot into the pile of the carpeting, aware that she was sounding defensive rather than confident and independent as she had planned, and she sensed rather than saw Massimo nod in response.

"I see," he said. He seemed to be trying to control a hint of amusement in his voice. "I'm sorry that I offended you. But as for not leading anyone on... well, perhaps not intentionally..."

Jenny glanced up quickly, long enough to see Massimo shaking his head and grinning broadly, then settled her gaze back on the carpet.

"I'm afraid I fail to see what's funny," Jenny said grimly. This was not going at all as she had planned. She set her jaw in determination, still staring at the rug. "But what I really came to talk about was where we stand, Massimo. You . . ." She kicked one foot lightly against the other. "You made love to me last night, and then you ran off to Milan. I want to know why."

When Massimo answered, his voice was no longer amused. "Milan has nothing to do with you, Jenny. I have told you that."

Jenny felt her lips tighten. "You won't discuss it?"

"There is nothing to discuss."

"Well . . ." She wanted to turn on her heel, to tell him that in that case there was nothing to discuss between them at all, ever again. But she felt somehow rooted to the little square of carpet where she stood, watching her bare toes in the moonlight.

"And what else?" Massimo asked. His voice had relaxed slightly.

Jenny's anger ebbed and flowed, focusing now on Massimo, now on herself. Just a few minutes ago in her room, she had been so sure that she could march in here and say, "Now see here, Massimo, I want to know about this Miriam person, and I want to know why you've been behaving irresponsibly with Gabriella's money." But now, with a half-naked Massimo sitting there smiling at her, her voice seemed simply to desert her. She blinked hard.

There was a movement by the window, and suddenly Massimo was within her field of vision, down on his hands and knees on the rug in front of her. He picked at a spot by her foot with his hand, pulling up tiny tufts of carpeting and examining them critically.

"Massimo!" Jenny cried, half in alarm. "What on earth are you doing?"

He looked up at her, holding a bit of rug in his hand. "Trying to figure out what interests you so intensely that you cannot look at me. The carpet is dirty, perhaps? Something crawls about in it? Rosa has not been too efficient lately?"

Jenny's mouth fell open in exasperation.

"Massimo," she began impatiently. But the corners of her mouth were turning up almost involuntarily. "It's not dirty, Massimo. There's nothing wrong with the rug."

Massimo rocked back on his knees, folding his arms over his chest and looking at her steadily from below. "Ahhh. Then you must be *avoiding* looking at something." He turned his head to look at the windowsill where he had been sitting. He frowned in concentration, then suddenly snapped his fingers. "The moon!" he cried. "The moonlight was in your eyes, perhaps?"

Jenny glared at him, trying to look stern, but she couldn't do it. "Massimo, you look ridiculous. Get up off your knees, and for Lord's sake, put a shirt on!"

Massimo started to rise, but a grimace of pain crossed his face. Jenny reached a hand instinctively for his shoulder.

"Massimo!" she cried softly. "Are you all right?"

"It's my knee," he whispered, his eyes closed.

Jenny sank down to her own knees. "Is it all right?" she said anxiously. "What can I do?"

His eyes remained closed, but he reached out both hands and grasped Jenny's arms for support. "It's nothing, really, an old football injury."

Jenny's eyes narrowed. "Football? Where did you play football?"

His hands tightened on her arms. "Oh, Jenny, it's just one of those things that comes and goes. Perhaps if you could massage it a little . . ." Something was making the corners of his mouth twitch.

"Massimo," Jenny said more firmly, "where did you play football?"

He opened one eye and looked at her. "An old war wound?" he said tentatively.

"Massimo," Jenny said, "there's nothing wrong with your knee, is there?"

Massimo's eyes opened, an expression of hurt in them. "You don't believe me, Jenny? You don't believe that I'm in pain?"

Jenny shook her head vigorously. "Not a word."

Massimo grinned, and it was the same dazzling, enchanting grin that Jenny had first seen at the Milan train station. The deep creases in his cheeks disappeared, and his whole face took on an open softness. He moved his hands on her arms, making small, gentle circles over her shoulders.

"But I am in pain," he said softly. "I am in pain with wanting you, Jenny." He pulled her close against his chest, and she could feel his heart beating through her breasts as they were crushed against him.

Thoughts tumbled through Jenny's mind. She had not come here to make love again; she had come for an explanation. But here they were, kneeling on the blue rug, holding each other. The moonlight was making shifting patterns on the carpet, like the sun on Mediterranean waves. Massimo's naked chest and shoulders gleamed in the silvery light, and she could feel the hard muscles of his back beneath her hands.

"Oh, Massimo," she whispered, "this isn't what I wanted."

Massimo tangled one hand in the thick mass of her hair and pulled her head onto his shoulder.

"Then what is it that you want, *cara mia?*" His voice was low in her ear. "What do you want from me?"

Jenny shook her head against his shoulder, nuzzling into the hollow of his neck. She could feel the heat of his skin against her lips and cheek, and she shivered from it. His mouth played at her ear.

She knew what she wanted. She wanted to hear him say, "I love you." But that seemed too much to ask. Much too much.

"I don't know," Jenny murmured.

Massimo's lips traced a fiery line down the edge of her jaw, brushing tiny kisses against the tender skin. He lifted her chin gently with one finger and let his mouth rest against her throat. His lips remained there for an eternity—an eternity that Jenny's mouth yearned for the feel of his—and all the while his hands were at work, the side of one thumb stroking her cheek and the other moving lazily up and down her side. Jenny felt desire rising in her as slowly and powerfully as a wave rises from the depths of the ocean, pulled by the tide, reaching for the moonlight and the endless heavens.

Finally Massimo raised his head, and his mouth met hers in a kiss that was first delicate, then urgent. His hands slid to her waist, beneath the hem of her sweater, and with a movement that was almost unconscious Jenny broke the bond of their lips long enough for him to pull the sweater up and over her head, to lay it neatly on the carpet beside them, and to slide the wisp of silky cloth that held her breasts off over her arms.

Massimo's eyes were wide and golden as they explored Jenny's nakedness. His hands grasped her arms with an intensity that would have hurt had she not welcomed his demanding touch. She returned his passionate fascination, letting first her eyes and then her fingertips range over his chest, his throat, the planes of his face. She ran her hands lightly over his ribs and heard him suck in his breath as her fingers toyed with the tender flesh around his nipples. Her own breasts were stretched taut, painfully so, eager for his touch.

Massimo shook his head in wonder. "Jenny, you are even more beautiful than I realized. Last night, in the darkness . . ."

Jenny put a finger to his lips. She had wanted to talk, but now she wanted only silence, only the sweet, soft murmurs of desire.

She let her fingers trail downward again, over the

cordlike muscles of his neck and shoulders, down his chest as it rose and fell with his quickened breathing, stopping at the hardness of his waist to massage the tight muscles, then down again, her fingers slipping inside the waistband of his tailored slacks. Her hands rested there as she leaned forward on her knees, and she let her mouth follow the trail of her hands, planting little, burning kisses over his neck and shoulders, his chest, the sensitized flesh just above the waist.

This time, Jenny knew, *she* was leading them forward. She felt a giddy delight in what she was doing. Slowly, her hands undid the fastenings of his slacks and slid the fabric down over his hips. His hands echoed the motions of her own. In what seemed like one harmonic movement, the two of them removed the last barriers between them.

The rest was a gentle process. Massimo lay back on the blue carpet and Jenny knelt beside him. He smiled at her as his hands circled the heaviness of her breasts and stroked the soft flesh of her belly. She watched his face, fascinated, as her own hands moved about his body; watched his mouth part slightly, his eyes widen, heard his breath quicken.

Then he circled her body with his arms and pulled her down to him, molding the full length of her body to his. Jenny rested her hands on his shoulders and let her knees drop to the carpet on either side of him, feeling him moving beneath her in gentle, rhythmic motions. She lowered her cheek to his, resting against him, and gathered a handful of his straight, black hair. She liked the feel of it against her palm.

Jenny could feel the eager hammer of Massimo's heart beating against her own breasts, pressed close to his chest. With a suddenness that startled them both, she slid her hands beneath his hips, closing the space that remained between them. An easy warmth flooded through her, like an early spring rain, and she smiled at him with eyes wide with pleasure and satisfaction.

He gazed back at her, his golden eyes drinking her into their depths. His face seemed sculpted from gold in the moonlight, like some ancient Egyptian mask. Jenny raised a hand and wiped a tiny line of sweat from his forehead; she pushed the heavy black hair back from his brow.

"You are a remarkable woman, Jennifer Armstrong," Massimo said softly. He kissed her lightly, holding her head between his hands and bringing her face down gently to meet his own. "I am overwhelmed by you. I need you."

Jenny smiled at him sleepily. Remarkable, overwhelming. Necessary. But not loved. What would it take to make him love her, she wondered idly. What would it take to steal him away from the pale, perfect Miriam?

She slid off his body and onto her side on the carpet, resting her head in the crook of her elbow. Wasn't this enough for her? She had thought so last night. Massimo rolled onto his side as well and lay facing her, his elbow planted on the rug and his head propped in his hand. His face seemed rounder, somehow; it reminded Jenny of Luca.

"Why were you so angry about my seeing Luca?" she asked suddenly.

Massimo's expression didn't change, but it seemed to harden slightly. "Why were you with him?" he asked in return.

Jenny waved a hand in dismissal. "He just turned up after work. It was nothing. Just someone to talk to about . . ." Her voice trailed off as she remembered what they had talked about: her troubles with Massimo, Massimo's irresponsibility toward Gabriella . . .

"About what?" Massimo asked, running a finger around the rim of her ear.

Jenny shrugged one shoulder. "Oh, nothing. About work."

Massimo nodded. His face was sober, and he avoided her eyes. "I'm sorry about my anger," he said softly. "I know that nothing happened between you, and you were right in what you said when you first came in here. I was not being fair. But..." He took a deep breath and let it out slowly. "It seemed somehow like history was repeating itself."

Jenny looked at him in confusion. "I don't understand."

Massimo was silent for a moment, then suddenly he sat up. "I'm getting cold down here," he said with a little laugh. "Come. Come to bed with me."

He slid his hands under her elbows and pulled her up with him, holding her against him. Then he pushed back the covers on the big bed and lowered her gently onto it. Jenny started to sit up again.

"I should go back," she protested.

But Massimo's hands were firm against her shoulders, holding her against the soft sheets.

"Stay with me," he said gently. "Please."

Jenny relaxed against the pillow, and Massimo climbed in beside her, settling the thick, woven cover around them both.

"Now, tell me what you talked about with Luca. About work. I want to know how you're getting along with Gabriella."

"You're changing the subject," Jenny said accusingly.

Massimo shrugged. "You changed it first. Tell me."

It felt safe and comfortable in Massimo's big bed, with the heavy covers pulled up over them to their necks. And after all, Jenny told herself, she *had* wanted to know, to confront him with her doubts about him.

"Well, I'm sure it wasn't anything," she began weakly, "but Gabriella was kind of angry about some bill that hadn't been paid." Jenny began tracing little patterns on the sheet with one finger. "She seemed to think it was your fault."

Massimo's hand, which had been moving slowly up and down on Jenny's side, stopped abruptly. *"My* fault?"

"Well, she said something about...that stupid Silvano." Jenny ducked her head under the covers. "So I guess she meant you." Her voice was muffled by the heavy weaving.

"So," Massimo said. "This is what you told Luca. And what did Luca say in reply?"

Jenny tried to remember. "I can't really think. He didn't say much at all."

Massimo lay back on his pillow and laughed. "Well, I would expect no more, I suppose. And that does explain my message from *Mamma.*"

Jenny peeked back out at him. "Mamma?" she asked, wide-eyed. "Gabriella said something about calling someone's mother, but no one would explain what she meant. And Luca, I remember now, he just sort of avoided the question."

"Oh, it's our mother, all right," Massimo said.

"But what on earth does your mother have to do with Gabriella's finances?"

"My mother has to do with everything," Massimo replied with a chuckle. "And she wants to see us all for lunch tomorrow, which means something serious is on her mind. I had no idea what it was until now."

Jenny propped herself on one elbow and stared at Massimo. He rubbed his eyes with his knuckles like a little boy.

"You mean to tell me that your *mother* really runs the great *Società* Silvano?" Jenny asked incredulously. "No wonder you sometimes act like you've had enough of independent women!"

"No, no." Massimo was laughing hard now. "She doesn't run the *Società;* I do that. But she runs the family. And Gabriella's finances are family business." Massimo turned on his side and looked at Jenny, a grin on his face. *"Mamma* is much like you, in fact. Very smart, always wanting to be in charge—even quite fierce sometimes!"

Jenny stuck her tongue out at him.

"La padrona, we call her," Massimo said.

"What does that mean?"

"Oh . . ." Massimo thought for a moment. "There's really no translation. Boss-mother, maybe!"

Jenny rolled her eyes. "She sounds a little scary."

"No, not at all. She is really quite wonderful. As I say, sometimes very much like you. Like Gabriella, even more."

The mention of Gabriella brought a frown to Jenny's face. "Well, what *did* happen with Gabriella's bills, Massimo? How could you let that happen to such a good friend?" She picked at the woven cover with one finger. "Maybe more than a good friend, according to Luca."

Massimo rolled quickly onto his side, propping his head on his hand. "Luca said that? That there was something between me and Gabriella?"

"Well, you remember that first night at dinner. And then a couple of other times . . ."

"And you believed him?"

Jenny smiled. "Oh, Massimo. Luca is such a little boy. I don't think he knows *how* to tell a lie. But I suppose he could have been teasing . . ." Jenny looked at Massimo with steady eyes. "So there is nothing between you and Gabriella?"

Massimo drew his fingers across his chest. "Cross my heart. There is a long and close friendship—and it is true that *Mamma* would have liked to make a match. But Gabriella has always—since she was born, almost—known what she wanted. She runs her life absolutely; she is married to her career. She seems sometimes confused, but believe me, she is not. I like her spirit." He smiled gently at Jenny. "She is full of life. But I prefer to help out my woman just a little bit, now and then. To buy a train ticket for her, perhaps . . ." His smile was mischievous now, and Jenny returned it.

"And about the unpaid bills," Massimo went on, "that is not my fault, nor the fault of the *Società*."

Jenny looked at him closely. "Well, whose then? Why did she call you that stupid Silvano?"

"Are you sure she meant me?"

"Who else?"

Massimo touched the tip of one finger to her lips. "I think you wouldn't believe me if I told you. So you must come tomorrow."

"Tomorrow?" Jenny started to sit up, but Massimo drew her close to him, his hands on the small of her back.

"Tomorrow you shall meet *Mamma*."

"Don't be silly, Massimo." Jenny shook her head. "That's obviously a family gathering. I'm not invited."

"I'm inviting you," Massimo said firmly. "And you shall come. That's the only way to make you understand—and believe. But for tonight, we have other things to do."

Chapter 7

AN INSISTENT POUNDING intruded on Jenny's consciousness. She rolled over on her side and opened one eye. The little alarm clock was just outside her field of vision, but it had to be the middle of the night; it seemed like only moments ago that she had left Massimo's room.

The pounding persisted. It sounded like someone beating a kettle drum just beside her ear. Finally a high-pitched voice was added to the din.

"Jenny! Jenny, *prego,* can I come in?"

Jenny pulled the covers over her head and tried to tell herself there was no one there. But the noise refused to stop.

"Jenny!"

Jenny flung the covers back from her face and glared at the door. "Angela," she responded in something like a growl, "what on earth are you doing up? It *can't* be morning yet."

The door burst open, and Angela, red-gold curls bobbing, flew into the room.

"Si, si, Jenny, is nine o'clock already! And we go to *Nonna's* today, to the big house! And you are coming, too, *Papà* says so. Come on, Jenny, get up, get up!"

Angela bounced up and down next to the bed with an energy that appalled Jenny.

"To *Nonna*'s?" she asked sleepily, playing for time. "Who's that?"

Angela looked exasperated. *"Nonna!"* she almost shouted. "Is Grandmamma, yes? Come *on*, Jenny!"

"Ummm," Jenny muttered. She cocked one eye toward the clock. It did indeed say nine o'clock. What had happened to the night? She had no idea what time it had been when she had struggled into her clothes and back to her own bed, leaving Massimo despite his entreaties that she stay.

"Angela, *cara*, it's much too early to do anything. I was up . . . very late last night." She felt the beginnings of a blush in her cheeks, and she pulled the coverlet up around her face.

Angela shook her head and looked unhappy. "No, no," she cried, "you *have* to get up. *Papà* says so. *Papà* says we must leave soon!" She pulled anxiously at Jenny's arm through the covers.

Jenny stared at the little girl for a moment longer, shaking her head slowly. "How can you be so wide awake?" she asked with a yawn. Then she blinked her eyes rapidly, ridding them of the last traces of sleep, pushed the bedclothes away, and reached over her head in a mighty stretch. Angela clapped her hands excitedly at these signs of life.

"Okay," Jenny said finally. "if *Papà* says so, it must be true. I'll be ready in half an hour. Now scoot!"

Angela looked at her quizzically. "Scoot?" she repeated.

"Out! Out!" Jenny waggled her hands at the little girl. "Let me have a bath. And tell *Papà* I'll be there. Don't worry."

Angela nodded, but she didn't look convinced. "You are up now, for sure?"

Jenny laughed. "For sure. Honest." She swung both

legs over the side of the bed in confirmation. "See?"

Finally grinning, Angela turned and headed out the door at a run, eager to report that all was well in this quarter.

Left alone, Jenny sighed and padded to the bathroom. Ten minutes in a hot, bubble-filled tub went a long way toward making up for her lack of sleep, and when she emerged, wrapped in an immense, midnight-blue towel, she felt almost cheerful about the day to come. After all, Massimo had promised that her questions about the financial dealings at Gabriella's would be answered, and that might mean one less doubt she would have to wrestle with in her love for him. Of course, there would be *Mamma*...

By ten, bathed, dressed and full of scrambled eggs and *prosciutto* from Rosa's kitchen, Jenny was ready to go. Nino had eaten with her, talking animatedly about the good times they would have at *Nonna*'s house, and his excitement was infectious. He was still chattering when Massimo and Angela joined them in the little foyer.

"Is it really so wonderful at *Nonna*'s?" she asked Massimo good-naturedly.

"Ah, *si, si!*" the two children cried in unison. But their father shrugged. A smile lit his sharp features, and the gold in his eyes glowed softly.

"That will be for you to decide," he responded.

The drive down the coast to Rapallo was even more beautiful than Jenny had imagined it might be. As Massimo drove the gray car out through the western suburbs of Genoa, a perfectly clear blue sky wrapped them in warm, vaguely moist air, and the brilliant sun lent a silvery shimmer to everything. At the boundary of the city itself, the plain separating sea and mountain narrowed to the width of a few blocks, and a single main road led along the coast. Off to their right, the Mediterranean sparkled in shifting patterns of blue and white and silver. For a brief while, a stately white cruise liner held even with them as it pulled out of Genoa harbor.

"Heading for Venezia," Massimo said, gesturing toward the ship. Jenny glanced at him, and he was smiling. "The only way to arrive properly in Venice—by ship. Very romantic."

Jenny raised one eyebrow. "It sounds wonderful," she agreed. "And how many times have you done it?"

Massimo was quiet for a moment. "I went once by ship with my parents, when I was very young," he said finally. "I thought to go again by ship, with my wife, after our wedding. But..." He shrugged. "She preferred Monte Carlo. She did not much like Venice. Of course, I have been many other times as well, by train or by plane, but it is not the same."

"I can't imagine not liking Venice!" Jenny cried impulsively. "I mean..." She bit her lower lip. "I don't mean to be critical; I'm sure your wife had reasons for her opinion. And of course, I've never been there at all—not by air or by train, let alone by ship! But it's always seemed like such a magical place to me."

"It is," Massimo agreed, his eyes steady on the winding road. "Magical. Perhaps..." He glanced at Jenny slyly. "Perhaps we can go there one day."

Jenny stared out the window of the car toward the tiny whitecaps that dotted the sea. She could feel a warmth in the back of her neck; she wasn't sure if it was the heat of the sun, or her consciousness that Massimo was watching her with dark, hooded eyes that darted back and forth from the road to her.

Suddenly the children, who had been arguing quietly in the back seat, flared at one another, and Jenny was grateful for the responsibility of sorting out their differences. She felt neither able nor willing to give Massimo a response.

The road hugged the coast for some miles, then pulled inland to circle behind massive Portofino Mountain, a rock bluff that jutted half a mile or more out into the sea. Finally they swung back toward the coast to enter the resort city of Rapallo.

"This is where the Silvanos really live," Massimo said as he maneuvered through the wide boulevards and into the open plaza that overlooked the port crammed with sailboats. "It is the family's summer home, actually. But *Mamma* prefers it to the city. She comes into town only for the worst winter months, when this part of the coast is very damp and cold."

"Did you grow up here then?"

"*Si*, this was my home as a child."

They drove on out of the city itself onto a wide spit of land that formed the harbor. For a while they followed a small lane, guarded on both sides by high stone walls. Then Massimo turned the car in through an arching, wrought-iron gate. At first, Jenny couldn't see any buildings at all. The curving drive was lined with immensely tall, stately cypresses, and beyond the land was wooded and thick with underbrush. Then finally a break in the trees revealed a large white stucco house.

"It's lovely!" Jenny exclaimed.

Massimo chuckled. "I'm afraid that is my cousin's house," he responded, obviously amused. "And the next one you see, that will be my sister's. There are several houses on the compound for our family."

Jenny glanced at him sharply. "Your sister?" she asked pointedly.

"*Si*. I have one older sister. She lives most of the time in Milano, with her husband. But she keeps her house here."

Jenny felt a tiny stab of pain behind her eyes at the mention of Milan. But she kept her mind on the question at hand.

"Have you any other family I don't know about?" she asked.

Massimo shook his head. "No more." He nodded toward a blue house off in the distance—the third they had seen. "That was supposed to be mine. But I found that sometimes the children and I like to have not quite so much family. So we have a summer home in Portofino. Besides, there is room for us at the main house."

They rounded one more curve in the drive, and the rows of cypresses ended abruptly. Jenny's eyes widened. Before them was a fantasy of pale green stucco, its myriad windows shuttered against the late morning sun. It was out of a picture-book—an elegant, classical Mediterranean *villa*.

"So, this is your little log cabin," Jenny said ironically.

Massimo nodded, smiling, as he pulled the car to a halt on the circular gravel drive in front of the massive white double doors. "My humble home," he said. "I hope you approve."

Jenny dipped her head in amusement.

Angela and Nino were out of the car almost before it had stopped, and at the same moment one of the double doors swung open. Two women emerged into the bright sun. One, almost a twin sister to Rosa, wore the same snowy white apron and beamed broadly. The other was tall and stately, a reflection of the cypresses and of the *villa* itself. Her hair was silver, and her eyes were of the same mysterious darkness as her sons'.

Jenny took a deep breath and wiped her hands slowly on the soft fabric of her slacks. *Mamma* was impeccably dressed in a matching skirt and sweater of a green slightly darker than the house itself; she wore spectator pumps, and her legs, Jenny noted admiringly, looked like those of a twenty-year-old.

The children kept their grandmother occupied with hugs and chatter for the moment it took Jenny and Massimo to climb out of the car. Massimo slipped a hand under Jenny's elbow.

"Don't be nervous," he whispered softly in her ear.

Jenny pulled her arm away. "I'm not nervous in the

least," she hissed back at him. "Why should I be?" The
smile on her lips felt tight and slightly unreal to her.

Signora Silvano advanced toward them as the other
woman—Rosa's twin—shooed the children on into the
house. She held out a hand to Jenny and smiled coolly.

"How do you do, Miss Armstrong?" she said, her
voice deep and confident. "Massimo told me you would
be joining us today. I am so pleased to welcome you to
my home."

Jenny wondered if she looked as uncomfortable as she
felt. She shook the older woman's hand—too vigorously, she told herself unhappily—and smiled at her
brightly. "I'm delighted to be included. Thank you for
inviting me!" What a stupid thing to say, Jenny thought
immediately; *she* didn't invite me at all. She probably
doesn't even want me here!

Massimo quickly leaned forward and planted a kiss
on his mother's cheek. *"Ciao, Mamma.* Everything is
well with you?"

Signora Silvano waved a hand in a gesture of disgust.
"Eh," she said with a shrug, and Jenny suddenly remembered with amusement that Stefania had used exactly the
same combination of word and gesture the day before.
"As well as can be, with this difficulty . . ." She glanced
at Jenny, then back to Massimo.

"Jenny knows that we have business to discuss,
Mamma," Massimo said lightly. "But perhaps first we
can relax. I'm sure our guest would like to see the house,
and until the others arrive, there is little we can do."

"Ah, of course, where are my manners?" The *signora*
turned to Jenny and put a hand on her arm. "I'm sorry,
my dear. Please, come in."

Inside, the house was even more impressive. The central hall, marble-floored and with curving staircases rising on either side, had a back wall of glass doors, and
through them Jenny could see a broad stone terrace and
a vast expanse of green lawn sloping down to the sea.

At the foot of the lawn, a tall-masted sailboat was tied to a small dock.

The foyer was vaguely intimidating, its ceiling rising the height of the *villa,* like something out of a movie set, but the room into which the *signora* led them next was nothing like it except that it, too, had glass doors along its rear wall. Small and well proportioned, it was a cozy sitting room with thick Persian carpets and chintz-covered chairs. The most noticeable thing about it, however, was its quantity of flowers. Fresh flowers in vases were set on every table and bookcase, paintings of flowers graced the walls, floral-patterned cushions were arranged on the sofas and chairs.

"This is beautiful!" Jenny cried impulsively, and she was rewarded by the first real smile she had had from *Signora* Silvano—a smile as dazzling and enchanting as Massimo's, and one that transformed her elegant face in just the same way. Jenny felt a sudden release of the tension that had been growing in the pit of her stomach. She nestled comfortably into one of the overstuffed chairs. Massimo, catching her eye, gave her a wink that made her smile broadly in spite of herself.

In only a few minutes, Rosa's twin—who was, it turned out, actually Rosa's older sister, and whose name was Maria—poked her head into the little sitting room and asked the *signora* to come and oversee the luncheon arrangements. Massimo rose from his chair and pulled open one set of the glass doors.

"Would you like to walk outside until lunch?" he asked. "The children are no doubt playing out here somewhere."

Jenny nodded and joined him at the door.

Bright blue and white cushioned chairs were scattered about on the stone terrace, and the lawn was manicured almost to a fault. Off to one side, with a small grove of shade trees beside it, was a swimming pool. The whole area was dotted with flower gardens, already in riotous color, and beyond shone the sea, blue and silver, with the tall sailboat bobbing on its tether.

"Well," Jenny said, trying to sound properly unimpressed, "it must have been quite a treat growing up here."

"Sometimes," Massimo agreed thoughtfully. "But sometimes it felt very . . . cut off." He gestured to either side of the lawn, where high stone walls shielded the property from the outside. Jenny remembered the gate they had passed through on the way in and wondered if it were usually kept closed.

"The whole compound is walled in," he went on, "all four houses. We played only with our own family, or occasionally with a neighbor like Gabriella." He shrugged and laughed lightly. "Wealth is not always a wonderful thing; especially, I think, for children."

"But your children seem very happy," Jenny protested. They could see Angela and Nino running races at the foot of the lawn.

"I work hard to make them happy," Massimo replied flatly. "Especially so since their mother died."

They walked in silence for a few moments, waving to the children when they caught their eye. Then Massimo went on: "I think sometimes that it was my isolation as a child that made me choose the wrong woman for my wife. For my . . . first wife."

Jenny glanced at him, but he was looking away, watching the children play. It was the first time she had heard him imply that he might marry again.

There was a double swing set in the little grove next to the pool, and they sat down, not touching one another but comfortable together.

"My mother and father, they always assumed that Gabriella and I would marry." He turned to look at Jenny, and the gold rims around his dark eyes glinted with amusement. "It is remarkable, sometimes, what adults do not see. Gabriella was a sister to me, not a wife. And

I was never more than a brother to her. When she finally made that clear to *Mamma*—when she borrowed the money to start her business—I was suddenly relieved of this great responsibility. And then I found this exotic creature who was Teresa, and I married her at once."

Massimo shook his head ruefully. "Perhaps if I had had more experience..."

Jenny looked at him sharply. "Experience is one thing you hardly seem to lack," she said.

Massimo nodded slowly at her, as if considering what she had said. "You believe that. Then there is much about me that you don't understand, *tesora mia.*"

Jenny's response was cut short by the appearance of Gabriella at one of the glass doors, shouting at them and gesturing them in for lunch. Massimo turned down toward the water to fetch the children, and Jenny went on ahead, to be greeted with a warm hug from Gabriella.

"Jennifer, I am so happy to see you here! Yesterday I was afraid you would run away and never return; I was so rude, so angry!"

Jenny smiled. "You weren't rude to me, nor angry at me."

"Then I am forgive?" Gabriella asked anxiously.

Jenny laughed. "Forgiven," she corrected. "And there's absolutely nothing for me to forgive, Gabriella. I just hope whatever the problem is can get sorted out."

"Ah, *si, si, la mamma,* she sort it out. You wait." Gabriella winked outrageously, screwing up one green-painted eye, then took Jenny by the hand. "Now, is time for lunch. Come."

They joined the *signora* in the elegant dining room off the opposite side of the central hallway, and Jenny noted with a certain awe the paintings on the walls. The china was creamy white with a tiny pattern of blue and pink flowers, and the silver and linens were quite clearly the real things. *Signora* Silvano looked comfortably at home amidst her expensive surroundings, and Jenny felt a twinge of uneasiness; this was not an environment where people would willingly take to a working girl. But Massimo had said that his mother was a lot like Gabriella—and, for that matter, a lot like Jenny herself.

Massimo and the children tumbled in through the glass doors and found their places with much giggling. The *signora*'s English was not perfect, and she was self-conscious enough to prefer not to use it. Angela and Nino lapsed quickly into their own language as well, and despite Gabriella's best efforts to include her, Jenny felt more and more left to herself. She kept a smile on her mouth, but the uneasiness slowly became something more—a kind of awkward certainty that she didn't fit in here. The kind of woman who would fit in here was Miriam, the lovely, pale Miriam.

When Luca, high-spirited and effusive, burst into the room halfway through lunch, Jenny felt her mood brighten immediately. She had almost forgotten that Luca was a member of the family, and she had not really expected to see him at this gathering, the purpose of which was business. Luca seemed to have very little to do with the business part of the Silvanos.

He planted a huge kiss on his mother's cheek.

"Mi dispiace, Mamma, a thousand apologies, I am so late! There was traffic, and I had other errands I must attend to..." Luca spread his hands wide in a gesture that suggested he could not possibly have gotten here sooner.

Signora Silvano returned his kiss coolly. Her smile was fond, but there was something sad about it as well. Jenny looked at her hostess curiously, then turned to glance at Luca as he found his seat. He looked vaguely nervous, as though he, too, did not quite fit in here. When she caught his eye, Jenny smiled sympathetically. They were the two odd men out, it seemed.

It was not until after lunch, with the children safely outside playing once again, that the real business of the day was brought up. The five of them retreated to the flowered sitting room and chatted politely until Maria had brought coffee and served them all. *Mamma* Silvano took a sip from her delicate blue and white cup, then put it carefully down in its saucer.

"So, Luca," she said, looking at her younger son. *"Mi dice* Gabriella . . ."

"English, *Mamma,*" Massimo broke in. "I want the *Signorina* Armstrong to understand."

Signora Silvano looked at Massimo, then sighed. "I will try," she agreed. She turned her attention back to Luca, and Jenny looked at them curiously. Why was she speaking to Luca? What could Luca possibly have to do with all this?

The *signora* cleared her throat and began again. "Gabriella has told me, Luca, that there have been problems for some months now. Bills not paid on time, money not getting where it is supposed to be."

Luca shrugged. "I am not so efficient as my wonderful big brother," he said lightly.

Jenny pressed her lips together and stared at him. Was she hearing this correctly? Were Luca and his mother saying that Gabriella's bills were *his* responsibility, not Massimo's?

Mamma shook her head vigorously. "No, *bambino mio,* this time it is not good enough. This time we cannot accept."

The red patches on Luca's cheeks darkened, and he glanced ruefully at Jenny, as if enlisting her support and sympathy.

"Mamma," he said, "it will not happen again."

"No," his mother agreed firmly. "It will not. This was the last time that we give you responsibility. We had hoped, Massimo and Gabriella and I, that because Gabriella is your friend, you would see this task with a greater sense of responsibility, but no . . ." *Signora* Silvano lapsed into rapid Italian, and suddenly Luca came

alive as well, rising from his chair to pace the room and
gesturing as he replied to his mother's charges. Gabriella,
sitting on Jenny's left, followed the conversation with
sad eyes and provided an occasional attempt at translation.

Jenny watched almost unbelievingly, her mouth slightly
open and her brow furrowed. She pushed at her hair from
time to time out of nervous habit. She sought Massimo's
eyes, but he was concentrating on the conversation, adding an occasional word to his mother's arguments and
finally speaking at length himself. For once, it was Luca's face that appeared closed and curtained, the eyes a
flat dull brown. Massimo's face was unusually animated
and open, even vulnerable.

Last night, when she had told Luca about the scene
at Gabriella's, he had sighed over Massimo's irresponsibility and let Jenny continue to believe in Massimo's
guilt for whatever it was that had gone wrong. Could it
be true that it had been Luca's fault all along? Jenny
shook her head briskly, as if to clear it of the confusion.

Finally the rapid-fire Italian slowed a little. The *signora* put her hand on Luca's shoulder and made what
seemed to be a final statement, and Luca replied with a
tiny shrug, almost a gesture of disgust.

"She say he will be simply on an allowance from now
on," Gabriella interpreted in a whisper for Jenny. "No
more things to handle. He will have to manage from his
own money, and not from other people's."

Jenny shifted her gaze to the tall woman beside her.
"You mean he was actually using your money for himself?"

"*Si, si,* that is what this is all about," Gabriella replied
in an impatient tone. "He has very expensive tastes, our
Luca. And he is a very charming boy. He thinks that
that is all he needs to be, charming. That that make up
for everything."

Something clicked in Jenny's head. Those were almost exactly the same words she had used the day before, in describing Massimo to herself. She looked at Massimo now, studying his face as he talked softly with Luca and his mother. Could she have been wrong about him in other ways, too? Was it possible that there were explanations for his occasional hard arrogance, his unpredictable rage the other night at seeing her with his brother—even for his relationship with the woman Miriam?

She was still watching Massimo but without really seeing him when she felt a touch on her arm and realized that Luca had left the conversation and was at her side. She turned abruptly to face him.

"Luca, how could you have let me believe..."

"Jenny, I am sorry," he interrupted. There was a look of little-boy chagrin on his face that brought a rush of sympathy to Jenny's heart. She pressed her lips together and waited.

"I am ashamed about last night," he went on, speaking in a whisper. Gabriella had joined Massimo and the *signora,* and the three were talking animatedly across the room. "I *meant* to tell you, but you seemed so convinced that it was Massimo's fault... and things are so very often my fault, that it felt..." He shrugged. "It felt a little nice to be able to blame Massimo for once."

Luca's eyes were wide as he gazed at her, unblinking, and Jenny felt a smile form itself on her lips. He was weak, and they were strong—and that was a situation she could hardly fail to sympathize with. She had been in it herself for years. She took his hand impulsively and gave it a quick squeeze.

Luca kissed her hurriedly on the cheek.

"I must leave," he said loudly, and the others looked up at him from across the room. "I am sorry for all this. Gabriella..." He took two steps toward her, and Gabriella nodded at him with a quick smile.

"It will be better this way, Luca," she said.

Luca returned her nod, then went to his mother and hugged her warmly. To Massimo he offered his hand, and his older brother shook it coldly, a look of impassivity on his carved face. His eyes were without emotion. Jenny looked at him narrowly. Of course, if Luca had continually disappointed him, his coldness was understandable, but still . . .

Gabriella said her good-byes almost as soon as Luca was out the door.

"Shall I call the children in?" Jenny asked, assuming that they, too, would be on their way shortly. She felt vaguely relieved that the day with Mamma was almost over.

Signora Silvano looked at Massimo. He was smiling his polite smile. *"Mamma* and I have one more matter that must be discussed, Jenny. I am sorry. Perhaps you would like to sit outside, on the terrace? There are books here, and magazines."

It was clear that she was being dismissed, that whatever was left to be talked about was even more private than the family's finances, more private than the younger son's irresponsibilities.

"Signorina Armstrong," added the *signora,* "you must forgive us, please. Another time, when you visit, I shall be more hospitable. We have suddenly many worries, our family . . ." She threw her hands out before her, palms up, and Jenny recognized the gesture immediately. "I hope you will forgive us; we are usually very polite people!"

Jenny nodded, smiling as best she could. "Of course," she agreed. "I'll be happy to wait outside. It's a beautiful day anyway."

She picked up two magazines from a nearby table. Massimo moved quickly to the glass doors and opened them for her; as she passed, she looked up at his face. He was watching her intently, something like confusion in his eyes. He lifted a hand and patted her gently on the shoulder, as though it were important simply to touch her. Jenny felt a surge of heat through her body at his touch. She stumbled slightly, and he grasped her arm, supporting her, then let go quickly as she found her footing again. They both seemed somehow awkward with one another all of a sudden.

Massimo left the doors standing open and stepped back into the room. Jenny shaded her eyes with one hand and searched the lawn for Angela and Nino, but they were nowhere to be seen. Perhaps they were with Maria, or playing in the woods. With a little sigh, she pulled one of the cushioned chairs around to face the sun, lowered herself into it, and began thumbing idly through one of the magazines.

It all seemed very confusing. The scene that had played itself out among the Silvanos and Gabriella should have answered some of her questions—and indeed it had. It had told her that she had been unfair to Massimo, blaming him for the troubles at Gabriella's. And it had confirmed Massimo's warnings about Luca; she had sorely misjudged him. And yet she was still confused. She wanted desperately to talk to Massimo, to sort out what had been said.

She looked up from her magazine and stared at the blue and silver sea. The sailboat brought to mind the dream that had haunted her since she had first met Massimo, and she permitted herself a smile as she remembered it: Massimo beside her in the cabin of a tall-masted sailboat, his coppery skin gleaming in the Mediterranean sun, only white swim trunks protecting him from her curious gaze. She chuckled to herself. There was really no doubt about it; she was in love with the man. She closed her eyes.

She could hear the murmur of conversation inside the sitting room through the open glass doors. Without meaning to, she began to try to translate; it was a habit she was acquiring in an attempt to improve her Italian. Suddenly one word pierced her consciousness, and she blinked her eyes open. Miriam. They were talking about Miriam. And they were talking in increasingly louder tones—having an argument of some sort.

Jenny stared at the sloping lawn before her, all her muscles tense, as she tried fiercely to comprehend more of what was being said. The *signora* was saying something about moral responsibility—words Jenny recognized from Mamma's earlier conversation with Luca. And she seemed to be asking Massimo what he intended to do.

Jenny realized with a start that her hands were clenched tightly enough about the arms of the metal chair to make the knuckles turn white. She eased her grip carefully, studying the hands as though they belonged to someone else.

So Miriam could not be explained away. She had a status in this family. She was discussed in terms of morality and responsibility; Massimo was required to *do* something about her. There was no possibility of dismissing Miriam as a casual mistress, one to be slept with and discarded. Like me, Jenny told herself grimly. A twinge of despair ran through her body. Perhaps the money problems were Luca's fault rather than Massimo's, but this—*this* burden could not be shifted.

Jenny shivered, and she looked up. Fluffy gray clouds were beginning to appear on the horizon, and the first of them had momentarily covered the sun.

Chapter 8

"So, NOW DO you understand about Gabriella's money?"

Jenny was staring out the window of the car, watching the shadows make patterns on the green mountains. She turned to face Massimo and nodded. "Why didn't you just explain it to me last night?" she asked.

Massimo smiled, keeping his eyes on the road ahead of him. "After what you said about Luca? That he probably didn't even know how to lie, such a little boy? Would you have believed me?"

Jenny looked at him thoughtfully for a moment. "I'm not sure," she admitted. "Maybe not."

"Luca has always been a little boy," Massimo went on. "For a long time, *Mamma*'s baby. She knows that she is partly responsible for what he has become. So are we all, probably. We all feel guilt."

"You sound as though he were some kind of monster!" Jenny broke in. "When all he really is is a little spoiled."

Massimo stared steadily at the road. "What he does to other people cannot be so lightly excused, Jenny, believe me." Despite the harshness of his words, Massimo's voice was sympathetic, and there was a softness to his face that suggested how much he cared for his younger brother.

"As you say, he seems such a little boy—how can he be dangerous? There is always one more person to be taken in by that charm, to give him what he wants." Massimo glanced at Jenny with a little smile. "Someone like you," he said.

Jenny was not amused. It had been a long and difficult day for her. She had learned, much to her chagrin, that she had misjudged Luca. And that knowledge brought with it a certain loneliness, for Luca had been her friend. Now she was on her own. She looked out the side window for a long moment, feeling a kind of bitter tiredness invade her body. Then suddenly she shifted to face Massimo again.

"I can understand Luca," she said sharply. "He's not the great financial genius, like his big brother, nor a picture of perfect elegance, like his mother. And heaven knows what his big sister is!"

"A lawyer," Massimo said, glancing at her with one eyebrow raised.

Jenny spread her hands before her in resignation. "A lawyer. Of course." They had been speaking in low tones so the children, almost asleep in the back seat, would not hear. But now Jenny's voice rose slightly. "All you people, so sure of yourselves, so confident—you can't possibly imagine what it's like to be *unsure* all the time, to think you're wrong every time you make a decision!"

A frown had replaced the little smile on Massimo's face. "You are not being objective, Jenny. Luca is not you—either as you were with Simon or as you are now. We have treated him with more kindness than you can possibly imagine. He has had second chance after second chance to work out his life—"

"Of course!" Jenny interrupted. "You treat him like a child, so he behaves like one. No wonder he has no sense of responsibility."

"Jenny!" Massimo's hands gripped the steering wheel so tightly that they were trembling. "It is not so simple, believe me. I had hoped that today would prove to you..." He stopped speaking for a moment as he maneuvered the car around a sharp curve in the road. "I had hoped you would understand," he said. He sounded tired. "It is not just money, Jenny. Luca also, in other ways...Luca was my wife's lover."

Jenny gasped. She stared at Massimo with wide eyes. "Oh, Massimo," she whispered. "I can't..."

"You can't believe it? So. It is true."

"No, no," Jenny said hurriedly. "I do, I believe you. It's just...No wonder you acted the way you did when you saw me with Luca. What you said, about history repeating itself..."

"Exactly," Massimo said. There was a dryness to his voice, as if he had long since shut out certain memories, certain pains. "And perhaps we should say nothing further. The children..."

The children chose that moment to make their presence known. The car was approaching the junction where they would turn inland, behind Portofino Mountain, and Angela suddenly shook herself awake.

"*Papà!*" she called from the back seat. "I have an idea—*meraviglioso!* We can go to our house for supper! We show Jenny our house, *sì, Papà? Prego, prego!*"

Massimo shook his head. "I'm sorry, *cara*, not today. We have had our adventure for today. We are all tired." Massimo glanced quickly at Jenny.

Jenny could hear a note of weariness in his voice that seemed beyond what he might feel from the day—a weariness born of many days. She looked at him curiously, wanting despite everything—despite what she had heard from the terrace—to reach out and comfort him.

Nino added his voice to the pleading. "But *Papà*," he cried, "we *need* to see the house—you said so just two days ago, *Papà!* You said that we must go soon to

Portofino, to check the house!"

"*Si, Papà, prego,* ple—e—ase!"

Jenny turned in her seat to look at the children, wide awake now and bouncing excitedly up and down. Massimo, Jenny knew, was hard put to resist any of Angela's requests, and so she was not surprised when he slowed the car.

"Jenny," he said uneasily, "would you mind if we drove by our own summer house, in Portofino? We needn't stop for long."

"No, no, *Papà,* we must stop and have supper there! We must open it up from the winter!" Nino shouted.

Jenny shrugged. There were too many big decisions to be made—decisions about her future, about her love for Massimo—and she didn't feel she needed to make this one, too.

"Whatever you like," she said.

Massimo swung the car off the main road, and they began winding out onto the great stone bluff. All around them was rocky woodland, but through the trees to the east Jenny could see the gray clouds she had first noticed in Rapallo, now larger and darker, hanging low over the sea. They drove on for half a mile or so, seeing nothing but woods and sky.

Then abruptly they emerged from the woodland, and below them was the tiny harbor of Portofino. The miniature, horseshoe-shaped port was almost unreal—too perfect to be true. Narrow streets wove among the handful of pastel stucco buildings, their red tile roofs gleaming in the sun, and the harbor itself was crammed full of huge sailboats and yachts. Massimo stopped the car at the crest of the bluff, and Jenny looked down. Between them and the village below, a dozen or more elegant *villas* dotted the sharply rising mountainside.

Jenny smiled. "No wonder you chose to live here," she said.

"It is a bit pretentious, actually," Massimo responded

with a shrug. "Too many movie stars. But we stay up on the hillside, and the children are happy here."

He started the car again. When they had covered about half the distance to the village, he turned the gray Fiat off onto a narrow lane, and the view was momentarily lost. Then, as suddenly as it had happened before, they emerged into a clearing that afforded another breathtaking vista of the port and its doll-house village.

In the center of the clearing was a rambling, old blue stucco house—not quite grand enough to be called a *villa*—with a lawn and garden to one side and a small covered swimming pool to the other. The house seemed to consist mostly of terraces—little ones outside the windows and a huge one at the back, overhanging the view of the port. The windows themselves were covered by solid white shutters, bolted against the now-past winter storms, and the house had a forlorn and deserted look about it.

Nino and Angela were out of the car even before the motor had stopped purring. They dashed here and there, inspecting the pool and the garden, running to the back to make sure the terrace hadn't crumbled in the four months they had been away.

Jenny studied the house. It had a charm, a ramshackle appeal that the great *villa* at Rapallo lacked.

"It's quite beautiful, Massimo," she said softly. "I can see why you love it here."

"Do you like it then?" he asked. She turned to face him on the seat, and he was looking at her with an intensity that was disconcerting. "My wife Teresa, she perferred the Rapallo house."

"I . . . I think I prefer this one," Jenny said, "at least from the outside." Massimo continued to study her face, and she felt a red flush settling in her cheeks. She turned away and looked back at the house.

"Could I see the inside?" she asked brightly in an awkward attempt to hide the confusion she was feeling.

There was something about the way he was looking at her... and the charmingly unelegant house... and the children standing at its big front door...

Massimo pulled a set of keys from the glove compartment, separating one large, old-fashioned one from the bunch, and got out of the car. They approached the house, and he twisted the large key in the massive brass lock on the front door. The door swung open with a creak.

"Is that the only lock?" Jenny asked incredulously, remembering the barred windows of her room at the Genoa apartment—not to mention the three locks on her apartment door in New York.

Massimo nodded, grinning. "That is one reason we like it here. This house is so..." He shrugged his shoulders. "Compared to the other *villas* here in Portofino, this house offers very few inducements to the casual thief. Anyway, we have a couple who look in on it during the winter."

They stepped inside. There was a vaguely musty smell; a second set of louvered shutters covered the windows on the inside, and the furniture was shrouded by white sheets. The children raced about, pulling off dust covers and pushing the shutters aside, flinging open windows. Jenny followed Massimo through an archway into a room that extended the whole length of the back of the house. She watched as he efficiently folded back wooden panels that covered the glass doors leading to the terrace.

Outside the sky was almost entirely overcast now, and the gentle, moist sea breeze had become more aggressive. The sea itself looked darker and heavier, almost leaden, and small waves were beginning to churn on its surface. Salt air blew in through the open terrace doors, quickly replacing the stale air of the closed-up house.

Massimo stood at the terrace doors looking out.

"Will it rain?" Jenny asked. "I saw the clouds at your mother's. But they seemed so far away. And I think I didn't really believe it could rain here in paradise."

Massimo laughed lightly. "How do you suppose paradise stays so green all the time?" he asked. "The rain comes up fast, especially here in Portofino, where there is sea on three sides. It is rather wonderful, sometimes, to watch it come."

"Jenny! *Papà!* Come see!" Jenny and Massimo exchanged quick smiles, then followed the sound of Nino's voice to the kitchen. There he and Angela were pulling bits of food out of a cabinet—two tins of sardines, a can of peaches, some coffee, one lone potato. Jenny looked over their scavengings with a critical eye.

"I expect we could do something with these, if you'd like . . . ?" She looked at Massimo questioningly. Unexpectedly, she found that she wanted to stay in this house. She wanted to sit and relax in one of the over-stuffed, cotton-covered chairs in the living room; she wanted to fix a meal for Massimo and his children in this small, inefficient-looking kitchen.

Massimo raised his black eyebrows and smiled. "I'm not sure I want sardine and potato stew," he said, making a face at them. "But there is a *rosticceria* just a few minutes down the path. I'll pick up some food—and perhaps you three can find some plates and things?"

"That would be lovely," Jenny said. She picked up the very old potato gingerly between two fingers and dropped it into a nearby trash can.

An expression of hurt passed over Angela's face. "But I *like* potatoes!" she wailed.

"Not that one!" Jenny and Massimo replied at the same time.

"But I shall get more, if you like," Massimo added with a laugh. He glanced out the window of the kitchen at the clouds. "And I'd better hurry. I'll be back in ten minutes."

Nino and Angela hunted down plates and glasses and silverware, dusty after four months of idleness, and washed them with the cold water that the kitchen faucet provided. Together they found placemats and napkins, and Angela ran outside for a moment and returned with a handful of early blooming primroses for the center of the table. By the time everything was ready, the sky outside had darkened considerably. Flicking light switches brought no answering burst of light; the electricity was still turned off. So Jenny sent the children to gather candlesticks while she rooted through drawers for candles and matches. She was lighting the last when Massimo appeared again, his arms loaded with packages. Like a magician, he pulled out a roasted chicken, containers of *fettuccine* with clam sauce, scalloped potatoes, and a mixed green *insalata,* a loaf of crusty bread, a bottle of mineral water for the children and one of red wine for himself and Jenny.

"Well, that should do," Jenny said with a smile.

She was remarkably, ravenously hungry. Massimo raised an eyebrow as she pulled two huge chunks off the loaf of bread, and she giggled. "I guess I didn't eat much at lunch," she said.

"Ah," Massimo replied with a nod. "Nervous, perhaps."

Jenny stuck her tongue out at him. "Nothing of the sort," she said firmly. The house in Rapallo, and the words she had overheard from the terrace, seemed very far away. The four of them, eating their little feast in this cozy house, seemed very ordinary and comfortable, as though they belonged together here.

Nino and Angela were so close to sleep by the time they had finished supper that Massimo, with a contented wink at Jenny, had no trouble lifting them gently onto the long couch in the next room and covering them with a blanket. Jenny leaned against the doorway watching as he stood by them, stroking their foreheads until he was sure they were sleeping soundly.

Then he moved quietly about the little sitting room,

pushing the louvered shutters together again and latching them, shutting out the vaguely eerie glow of the gathering storm. Jenny could see only his silhouette in the shadows. Behind her, the candles on the dining room table flickered and sputtered.

They cleared the table in silence, and Massimo washed the dishes while Jenny made coffee. From time to time Jenny glanced up to find him looking at her thoughtfully. She felt more at home at this moment, she thought suddenly, then she had ever felt in her life; and she said a silent, hopeless prayer that it could go on this way forever. If only there were no outside world, no Miriam.

They had just returned to the dining room with their coffee when the outside world intruded with a vengeance. The first huge drops of rain splattered loudly against the concrete terrace at the back of the house. With a quick glance at one another, they set their cups down and hurriedly moved from room to room, pushing windows shut and latching them against the storm. Even as they worked, Jenny could hear the wind picking up outside, and she closed the shutters to muffle the noise.

"Did you open the upstairs windows?" Massimo called from the next room as Jenny pulled the last shutter closed in the kitchen.

"I think the children might have; I haven't been up there!" Together, they raced for the stairs. At the top, Massimo led her quickly from room to room—the bright red and blue room that the children still shared, the pretty mauve and pink guest room, a book-lined study—closing windows against the ever-increasing wind.

The last room off the corridor was white, with small rust-colored rugs scattered about the floor. A clay fireplace was set into one corner in a style Jenny associated with the American southwest, and a platform bed, a small bookcase, and a comfortable chair with a lamp beside it were the only furniture. Jenny recognized it at once as Massimo's room.

The sky outside the open window was green and purple and black, the colors of an ugly bruise, and the outside shutters banged harshly against the walls of the house. Jenny hesitated for a moment on the threshold, and as she stood poised, a massive burst of wind blew a solid curtain of rain into the room. Instantly they were both at the window, heaving the glass panes shut with their shoulders, using all their strength against the force of the wind.

Massimo latched the window, but there was no way to reach the outside shutters. Their uncontrolled banging echoed like muffled drum rolls through the room, and the air almost shimmered from the greenish glow of the sky outside. Jenny stared at Massimo for a moment, her mouth open, then began to laugh.

"You're drenched!" she cried above the noise of the storm. "Look at you!" She reached a hand to his shirt and squeezed the sleeve; water cascaded to the floor.

Massimo shook his arms, watching with a bemused expression on his face as droplets of water flew off them in all directions. "I suppose," he said, smiling innocently, "that I shall have to change." He took a step forward. "Of course you have gotten a bit wet yourself."

Jenny looked down at her slacks and shirt—the same designer outfit she had worn on her trip to Genoa some days earlier, carefully cleaned and pressed in the intervening time by Rosa. She was dripping. Wide-eyed, she looked back at Massimo and pushed at her tangled mass of damp hair.

Massimo took another step toward her. With one hand he had begun unbuttoning his wet shirt; his smile was no longer innocent. Jenny felt a sense of rising panic. She wanted him desperately, with a strength that matched the raging storm. But she remembered the words she had heard from the terrace, her conviction that he could never totally belong to her, that she could never have more than part of him. His obligation was to Miriam . . .

Then suddenly there was no more time to think. A shudder raced through her body as Massimo pulled her to him, and the tension she had felt disappeared. She felt herself becoming liquid, fitting herself to him; they pulled off their wet clothes with a desperate urgency she had not felt before. The rain breaking with metallic clarity against the window and roof beat a frantic accompaniment to their need for one another.

They moved toward the bed together, their hands and mouths yearning to touch, to kiss, to explore each other. With motions made clumsy by desire, Massimo pulled off the sheet that covered the bed. Together they lay back on the bedspread, sighing with relief as their bodies entwined and their mouths met in a wild, searching kiss.

"Oh, Jenny," Massimo whispered hoarsely. "I need you so much."

She touched a finger to his lips, and his mouth closed over it for a moment, his tongue playing with the tip of it. But there was little time. There was a ferocity about their love that had not been there before, a ferocity that matched the fury of the storm outside. They drank each other in through their eyes and their lips and their fingertips, as though this had never happened before and might never happen again, as though they needed desperately to memorize every part of one another.

Shudder after shudder passed through Jenny as she felt Massimo against her—his harsh strength, the sharp lines of his face and body. She held him wrapped inside her arms and legs, wanting to make him part of her, and great rolls of faraway thunder punctuated the sound of their labored breathing. Finally they came together, and they both cried out in the urgent pleasure of it.

When it was over, they lay back exhausted. In silence, they watched through the latched window as the sky shifted color from purple and green to the thick gray-blue of a more ordinary evening. Massimo lay naked on top of the bedspread, his long lean body glistening with darkness and moisture. Jenny, leaning on one arm, traced the lines of his face tenderly with her fingers.

There was a chill in the air now from the storm and the night, and Jenny shivered. At once, Massimo was on his feet. He pulled open a closet door and then was back at her side, a heavy terry cloth robe in one hand.

"I am afraid there is only cold water," he said with a note of concern. "But if you would like to shower in that . . ."

Jenny nodded slowly. She felt a heaviness about her body that made all her movements slow; she was full of pleasure and love. Then she rose, gathered her clothes in one hand and took the robe in the other, and went into the little bathroom. She kissed Massimo's shoulder gently as she passed him.

The water was very cold indeed, and she stayed in the shower only long enough to rinse off. As she stepped out, Massimo was standing in the bathroom doorway, his pants on now but his chest still bare, watching her and smiling. He shook his head slowly as she used the terry robe to rub herself dry.

"I have never seen such beauty, Jenny," he said. "You are so full of warmth, so glowing with color . . ."

Jenny grinned and gave her head a shake, showering him with droplets of cold water. "Not so warm right now!" she said cheerfully. "And the color is undoubtedly the first sign of frostbite."

Massimo ducked his head playfully, then turned and went back into the bedroom. As she pulled on her own still-wet clothes, Jenny could see him, his back to her, putting on first his socks and then his shirt. She could see the soft linen of the shirt stretch taut against his back as he began buttoning it.

"Massimo," she called softly. "I want you to know something."

"*Si?*" he asked, still facing away from her, leaning over to tie his shoes.

"I want you to know..." She paused, not sure how to say what she wanted to say. "I want you to know that this is enough for me," she blurted quickly.

He continued to tie his shoes. Then slowly he straightened up. "This is enough for you," he repeated. He turned and faced her, but he was across the room from where she stood at the bathroom door, and she couldn't see the expression on his face. "I'm not sure I understand."

"I just mean that you make me so happy, I can ...manage things as they are."

"As they are," he repeated again. "I see."

Jenny was confused. She had been so sure, during her quick shower, that this was what he wanted—and that she could be happy with it as well. They were so wonderful together. And perhaps, sometime, she could even make him love her more than he loved Miriam. She had felt a confidence born of love. But he was acting so strangely now, not at all as she had expected.

She stepped tentatively back into the bedroom, still rubbing her hair dry with the terry robe.

"I'm not sure you *do* see; I'm not sure you know what I mean, Massimo."

"Yes, I think I do," he said. Jenny was close enough now to see his face. His eyes were curtained again, unfathomable, and the lines of his face were sharp. "We had best go see about the children." He turned abruptly and left the room.

Jenny stood for a moment longer, forlornly watching the place where he had been. She couldn't think what she had done, what she had said, to make Massimo withdraw into himself so quickly. Unless she had simply made him remember Miriam, made him remember that he had another, more important lover...

She finished drying her hair with fierce strokes, then slipped on her shoes and hurried down the stairs after Massimo. He had already carried the sleeping Nino to the car, and now he was lifting Angela into his arms.

He glanced at Jenny as she entered the little sitting room, motioned with his head for her to pick up their jackets and her purse, then moved quietly toward the front door. Jenny gathered up the things and followed him, pulling the heavy door shut behind her. She slid into the front seat of the car and waited while Massimo locked the door, gently maneuvered Angela into the back with Nino, and took his place behind the wheel.

They drove in silence for some miles. Thoughts tumbled over themselves in Jenny's head. It just didn't seem fair—any of it, all of it! Finally she took a deep breath.

"Tell me about Miriam," she said.

Massimo turned his head sharply to glance at her. "Miriam!" he repeated. "What on earth do you know about Miriam?"

Jenny shrugged. "I've . . . I've heard you talking about her—at dinner that first night, and today, at your mother's house . . ." Jenny stopped, unsure how to proceed.

Massimo shook his head firmly. "Miriam is a friend of mine, of our family. She lives in Milano. We . . . I . . . owe her certain obligations. She has nothing to do with us. Nothing at all."

"What sort of obligations?" Jenny asked rashly, hardly caring now whether or not she offended Massimo.

"It is nothing you need to know!" he said, whispering harshly. "I don't know why you think . . . I have certain responsibilities to her. There is nothing more to tell."

Jenny stared at him. How could he be saying these things—that Miriam had nothing to do with them—when it was clear that she had everything to do with them?

Suddenly Massimo snapped his head toward her again. "Don't you trust me, Jenny? Why can you not believe anything I tell you? Why must everything be proven to you?" His voice was hoarse with emotion. The car swerved slightly and slid briefly onto the wet gravel shoulder. Massimo quickly shifted his concentration to his driving and pulled the Fiat back onto the concrete.

It was a moment before he spoke again. "Miriam has nothing to do with us," he said again, his voice weary this time. "Please believe me."

Jenny continued to gaze at him, but he said no more. Finally she turned away and stared bleakly out the window as they drove the rest of the way home in silence.

Chapter 9

A PALE PINK coat lay across one of the straight-back chairs in the entrance foyer of the apartment, its satiny material gleaming softly in the dim light. Jenny hardly noticed it. She even dropped her own rust-colored jacket awkwardly on top of it as she tiptoed through, carrying the sleeping Angela to her room. Massimo moved quietly ahead of her, cradling Nino gently in his arms.

Later, when she returned to the foyer to pick up her jacket, the coat caught Jenny's eye. She looked at it blankly, a frown furrowing her forehead. It was not the sort of coat she would wear. It was made for a blond— a pale blond whose tastes ran to conservative, impeccably tailored clothes. A thought struck her with a force that was almost physical: it was the sort of coat Miriam would wear.

She was still staring at the coat when soft voices caught her attention. She looked up to find Massimo and Rosa coming into the foyer from the corridor. Massimo's dark head was bent toward Rosa; he was listening intently to her rapid murmurings.

"Massimo," Jenny said.

His head snapped up, and he looked at her almost

uncomprehendingly, as if he weren't quite sure who she was.

"Is someone else here?" Jenny asked softly, gesturing at the coat. She saw her hand tremble slightly and pulled it back quickly.

Massimo glanced at the coat, then back at Jenny. He shook his head briefly, and Jenny wasn't sure whether he was responding to her question or simply trying to clear his mind of confused exhaustion. She felt a tiny knot of panic forming in the pit of her stomach. She looked at Massimo intently, her eyes wide, willing him to send out some message to her. But his eyes were dull and tired; they told her nothing.

"I'm sorry, Jenny," he said finally. The creases along his cheeks were deepened by the shadows, and the muscles of his neck stood out like cords. His white shirt, still slightly damp from the storm, was wrinkled. "I must say good night now. I will see you in the morning."

With a small nod, Massimo turned back down the long bedroom corridor. Jenny watched him as he moved away from her. There was something—a sadness to the set of his shoulders, perhaps—that urged her to call to him. She raised one hand toward his retreating back. But then her eyes shifted back to the pink coat. She pressed her lips together and pushed at her hair with a suddenly angry hand. Miriam was here. There was no other explanation.

Jenny stood in the foyer for another long moment, breathing deeply, trying to control the rising feeling of sickness inside her. Then finally she followed Massimo's footsteps down the long corridor, turned into her own room, and wearily got ready for bed.

Sleep was a long time in coming. She stared wide-eyed at the ceiling, at the narrow line of yellow light from the streetlamp that outlined the shuttered window. When, eventually, her eyes closed, Jenny's dreams were haunted by images of the raging storm, powerful and frightening—and of those painfully devoted eyes in the photo on the piano.

She crawled out of bed the next morning feeling as though she had not slept at all. She knew she had; the clock read almost nine. But there was a heavy ache behind her eyes, and an emptiness in her stomach that had nothing to do with hunger. Briefly, she tried to pretend that she was simply tired, that there was no other cause for her misery. Then last night flashed quickly through her mind: the desperate, wonderful lovemaking; her impulsive decision to tell Massimo that she could be satisfied with only that; his unexpected withdrawal from her; and then the pink coat.

At least, she thought gratefully, it was Sunday. No need to go to work, to pretend that nothing was wrong. Something was most assuredly wrong. Jenny retreated under the coverlet and contemplated trying to sleep for another hour or two. The pillow felt seductively soft and the sheets comfortingly cool. Maybe by the time she woke up again, Miriam would be gone.

Then suddenly she sat up and pushed the covers aside angrily. Massimo had said they would talk today—and *this* time they would! He would simply have to tell her what was going on; he owed her that.

Her jaw set in determination, Jenny hunted through her closet for the brightest colors she could find—a kelly-green T-shirt, royal blue linen slacks and a bright yellow, lightweight cotton Chinese jacket. She brushed her hair into full, thick waves that framed her oval face and fell heavily below her shoulders. Defiantly, she rubbed plum-colored blusher onto her already pink cheeks. Massimo had said he wanted a woman full of life; that's what he would get!

She took one final look in the mirror, paused long enough to hook gold hoops through her ears, then strode out into the corridor and shut the door decisively behind her.

Massimo was not at the breakfast table, but the children were. Nino and Angela, and one other—a boy of about five, with the unmistakable dark good looks of a Silvano. As Jenny's eyes settled on him, she felt a stab of something in the pit of her stomach that she could identify only as pure terror.

"Jenny!" Angela cried as she entered the room. *"Buon giorno! Eccolo, il nostro cugino!"* The little girl was bouncing happily in her chair as she gestured at the unfamiliar boy.

Jenny looked at him, her mouth open slightly. *"Cugino?"* she repeated uncomprehendingly.

"Si, si! Il nostro cugino—la zia Miriam—"

"He is our cousin, Jenny," Nino broke in. He sent a disapproving look at his sister. "You have to speak English for Jenny, Angela."

"Your cousin?" Jenny asked, shaking her head slowly. It felt like a nightmare; she was still in bed asleep, and this must be a nightmare...

"Yes," Nino answered in his high, serious voice. "This is Carlo, our cousin. He is *zia* Miriam's son. They came yesterday, while we were away at *Nonna's*."

The little boy, who looked several years younger than Nino but slightly older than Angela, ducked his head shyly, then raised it and stared at Jenny. *"Buon giorno,"* he said softly.

Jenny returned his stare. He was their cousin, this boy—the son of their Aunt Miriam. But Miriam was not their aunt at all. She was their father's lover. It was as simple as that. And that made this little boy...

A tiny sound escaped involuntarily from Jenny. She reached for the back of a chair as her legs suddenly refused to support her. Nino was looking at her curiously, and even Angela seemed to sense that something was wrong.

"Jenny," Nino began, a worried look in his eyes. He

started to rise from his chair, but Jenny waved a hand at him and he sat down again, stiff-backed and tense.

"Buon giorno," Jenny whispered hoarsely. The words felt as though they would strangle her. Carlo's eyes stared back at her, and they were a flat, chestnut color. Then they opened wider, and she could see the faint hint of gold around their rims. With another small cry, she turned and fled from the room and then on out the front door of the apartment.

She walked quickly, almost blindly down the sidewalk, not knowing or caring where she was going. How monstrous! To bring his love-child into his own house, to pretend to his children that this was a cousin! How much did they know—Nino and Angela—about their father's relationship with their *"Zia"* Miriam? No wonder he felt certain "obligations" to that woman; no wonder he felt a "responsibility"! Jenny's eyes clouded with tears, and she let them fall unheeded down her cheeks.

Her steps slowed slightly as she approached the number 19 bus stop. She could hear the rasping motor of a bus behind her; impulsively, she turned and waved it down. Her breath came in gasps as she fell into a seat near the front, and her cheeks were damp with crying. She wiped at the tears with the back of her hand and forced herself to take in slow, deep breaths, trying to straighten out the thoughts that tumbled through her head faster than she could control or even comprehend them.

He was older than Angela, this little boy. And that meant . . . Jenny shook her head slowly, trying to deny the inevitable conclusion. Massimo's affair with Miriam had begun well before his wife's death. All his pained allusions to Teresa's unfaithfulness were colored now by Jenny's certainty that he had been unfaithful, too—that he had, in fact, fathered a son by his mistress.

Jenny pushed her tongue out the corner of her mouth and tasted the small, salty tear that had lodged there. Her hands were jammed in the pockets of her brightly colored jacket, clenched so tightly into fists that the nails bit painfully into her palms.

Suddenly she was aware that a man stood in front of her—had, in fact, been standing there for several moments. She looked up at him without curiosity.

"Scusi, signorina," he said, *"la tariffa, prego."*

Jenny studied him with blank eyes.

"La tariffa?" he repeated, slightly more forcefully.

Jenny blinked, abruptly realizing who he was and what he wanted, and at the same time realizing that she had come out with no purse, without any money at all. She felt quickly in the pockets of her jacket.

"Oh, signore . . ." She tried to think of the right words to explain that she couldn't pay the fare, that she didn't have the money, but her mind was a complete blank. *"Mi dispiace, signore, ma . . ."* Nothing. She couldn't even think of the word for money. "I . . . I don't have my purse!" she blurted finally, spreading her hands in frustration.

The man, who held a ticket pad in one hand, raised his cap slightly with the other hand and scratched his head. His face had taken on an expression of distinct disapproval.

"Signorina," he began again, but before he could say anything more, Jenny's tears, briefly under control, burst forth more rapidly and more abundantly then ever. With a gulp that turned quickly into a sob, she buried her face in her hands.

Through the noise of her own crying, Jenny could hear a variety of sounds. The conductor was making unhappy little clucking noises, and there was a murmur of sympathetic chatter from the other passengers. A hand patted her shoulder gently, and she looked up to find a dark, rather ferocious-looking woman holding out a big, white handkerchief to her. Jenny took it gratefully.

As she wiped self-consciously at her eyes, she was

aware that the woman and the conductor were huddled together, discussing something on which they obviously quickly agreed. The conductor returned.

"La tariffa, signorina," he said once again, and Jenny opened her mouth to try another explanation, but he waved her into silence. *"Non importa,"* he went on. *"Niente—va bene, va bene."* Then, with one more curious glance at her, he moved on to the other passengers.

Jenny felt silly. Crying in the privacy of one's own room was one thing; crying in the front seat of a public bus was quite another. She took a deep breath and finished drying her eyes, then glanced quickly around with a sheepish smile of apology. Most of the other passengers were pointedly looking in other directions or studying their newspapers, but the woman with the hanky returned her glance with a steely one of her own and nodded, as though this sort of thing happened to her all the time.

The bus pulled to a stop in front of the ruined opera house. Jenny stared at it blankly for a moment, hardly recognizing where she was. Then, with a little exclamation, she jumped up just as the driver pulled away from the curb, caught the door as it was slamming closed, pushed it open, and stepped down onto the sidewalk. She glanced back as the bus moved away from her and saw half a dozen curious faces studying her from behind the glass windows.

Gabriella. That was the thought that had come suddenly into her head. Gabriella can help. Jenny hurried around the corner, past the shell of the opera house and toward the now-familiar bright blue door of the House of Fortuna. But even as she approached it, her spirits dropped: it was Sunday. The likelihood that Gabriella was at the studio was slim. Still, she could think of no other place to go, no other friend . . .

The bell sounded shrill, as if it were echoing in an empty room. Jenny stuck her hands in the pockets of her yellow jacket again. She remembered her mood—defiant, confident—when she had picked her colorful clothes out of the wardrobe less than an hour earlier. Now their brightness seemed almost a mockery of her mood.

It was hot. The sun shone brilliantly in a perfectly clear sky, electric blue and crystalline. Jenny could feel a hint of dampness on her forehead, where her hair curled against it. She pushed the bell one more time in frustration, then turned and was partway down the steps when she heard the noise of the elevator whirring to a stop inside. Footsteps crossed the *terrazzo* floor, and the door was flung abruptly open.

"Sì, sì, chi è?" The expression of extreme irritation on Gabriella's long, almost horsy face faded immediately when she saw Jenny. *"Ma!"* she exclaimed. "Jennifer! You look terrible! What is happening, what is the trouble? Come, come in. *Dài, dài!"* She reached one long arm toward Jenny and enfolded her in it, almost pulling her inside the door.

"Oh, Gabriella, I'm so sorry—I've interrupted you. It's . . . it's nothing, really . . ." Jenny bit nervously at her lower lip, suddenly aware of what she must look like: her hair wild, her jacket wrinkled from the twisting of her hands in its pockets, tear streaks through the plum-colored blusher.

Gabriella pulled her mouth into a sarcastic frown. "Ah, of course, nothing." She nodded. "I can see from your face, is nothing at all. Come, come. We talk. You tell me."

A wave of relief swept over Jenny with almost physical force. "Oh, Gabriella, could we? I . . . I need someone just to talk to."

Gabriella nodded again, this time with a fierce vigor that threatened to dislodge her three-tiered brass earrings. "You need a friend. So. Here am I." She glanced around dubiously at the little reception room where they stood, then back at Jenny. "You have had breakfast? You have had coffee?" she asked.

Jenny shook her head forlornly.

"Then that is first," Gabriella said firmly. Jenny felt a wan smile on her lips; it felt good to have this remarkable woman taking control. Sometimes, she told herself ruefully, I *do* need other people to make my decisions.

Gabriella pulled open the front door which she had slammed shut just a moment before. Then she slapped a hand against her forehead. *"La chiave!"* she exclaimed. "I do this all the time. You wait here, just one moment. I get the keys."

Jenny stood on the front steps listening to the elevator as it made its slow progress up to the third floor and then down again. The sun, too bright even to have a color to it, lent a buttery glow to the ancient gray stone of the *palazzi* across the street, and their windows glittered like diamonds. The heat felt good, finally erasing the chill Jenny had felt deep within ever since that moment at the Silvano's breakfast table when she had come face to face with little Carlo. Or perhaps, Jenny thought, it was not the sun but Gabriella's cheerful warmth that was making her feel better.

Then Gabriella was back, a heavy brass key ring dangling from one hand and a purple shawl draped over her shoulders. She looked at Jenny critically, then laughed. "We make quite a pair, yes?" she exclaimed, fingering Jenny's yellow jacket and nodding her head at the bright blue and green of the rest of her outfit. Jenny smiled again, and this time it felt like a real smile.

Gabriella linked one long arm through Jenny's and headed down the block, through the remains of the original city gates and into *centro*.

"We go to my *caffè*," she said.

They walked quickly along the narrow streets, turning this way and that, and Jenny remembered her first adventure here, when she had gotten so very lost so very quickly. Today, perhaps because she was with Gabriella, the ancient city center seemed welcoming and friendly, a pleasant change from the colder, newer buildings. Jenny hurried to keep pace with Gabriella's long strides, her feet slipping occasionally on the cobblestones.

Gabriella's *caffè* turned out to be a lovely little place of dark wood and mirrors and spotless white tiles. A gleaming brass *espresso* machine stood on one of the counters, and an old wooden cash register with brass keys was on another. The glass cases beneath the counters were full of delicious-looking pastries: fruit tarts, puffs bursting with creamy custard, and things so dark with chocolate that, under ordinary circumstances, Jenny would have found them irresistible. Two waiters elegant in black jackets and bow ties and long white aprons greeted Gabriella with cheerful nods. Although the *caffè* was almost empty on this late Sunday morning, they spent several moments choosing the best table for their favored customer.

Without a word from Gabriella, one of the men deposited two steaming cups of *caffè latte* and a plate overflowing with pastries on the table in front of them, then withdrew to a tactful distance. Gabriella studied the pastries intently, finally selected one filled with raspberry jam, and bit off a large chunk. After she had washed that down with coffee and smiled contentedly at the anxious waiter, she finally turned to Jenny.

"Now," she said decisively. "You must tell me everything. From the start."

Jenny took a deep breath and complied. She felt no reluctance, as she had with Luca. She began with the first meeting at the Milan train station: her annoyance and then fascination with the remarkable-looking stranger who had so peremptorily solved her difficulties; their sudden discovery that she was to be his houseguest; her growing intuition that he was as attracted to her as she was to him.

Gabriella listened thoughtfully, chewing on one pastry

after another and calling now and then for another cup of *caffè latte*. She smiled when Jenny mentioned her misunderstanding about Massimo's relationship to Gabriella herself, and she shook her head soberly when Jenny explained how she had assumed that it was Massimo who had mishandled Gabriella's affairs.

"I know I'm not as open as I might be to a new relationship," Jenny admitted, "because of the way my husband treated me. I was . . . reluctant to start something with another man who seemed so strong and sure of himself."

Jenny gazed at her coffee, rich with steaming milk. "And then I couldn't be sure . . ." she went on, pausing for a moment to take a sip. "He seemed so unpredictable. I was never sure how he felt about me."

Gabriella nodded. "Massimo, he seems very strong. And he is, in some ways. He is a brilliant businessman. But with women . . ." Gabriella shook her head and made a little clucking sound. "He has told you about Teresa?" she asked.

Jenny picked at the tablecloth with one finger. "Yes," she said softly.

"Massimo, he was madly in love with Teresa. He give her everything. And she give him . . ." Gabriella gestured disgustedly with her hand. "She was a, how do you call it, a witch!" she hissed. "She hurt him very badly."

Jenny looked at Gabriella curiously. "You care very much about him, don't you?" she asked softly.

Gabriella nodded fiercely. "He is like my brother. And he take care of everyone else, but no one take care of him." She grinned at Jenny, her wide, hearty grin. "But now, maybe he has someone."

Jenny stared at her hands. Did Gabriella know, she wondered, about Miriam?

"You say you are frightened of a new love," Gabriella went on. "Well, Massimo, he is frightened, too. He must be proved that women are not all like Teresa, running after every man who comes to them."

Jenny smiled wanly. "He was furious when he saw me with Luca one evening," she said softly.

"Ah!" Gabriella cried, pouncing on Jenny's words. "So he would be. Luca was one of Teresa's many lovers!" She screwed her face into an expression of extreme distaste. "It has taken all his strength to forgive his brother for that. That and . . . other things." She waved a hand in the air. "Myself, I do not make the effort."

Jenny nodded. "He told me about Luca and Teresa," she said.

Gabriella sat quietly for a moment, evidently thinking over all of what Jenny had told her. She finished off her fourth pastry, wiped her mouth with her napkin, and brushed the crumbs carefully off her hands. Then she looked at Jenny with a perplexed expression on her face.

"This is everything?" she asked.

Jenny looked down at her hands, then took a last sip of her own coffee. "Yes," she said finally, so softly that Gabriella had to lean forward to hear.

Gabriella shook her head. "So, then, what is the problem?" She held up one hand and began to tick off the things that Jenny had mentioned. "You are both frightened because of what happened in the past. But you recognize that. And now you understand about me and Massimo, and about the money business. You see why Massimo might be *un po' furioso* when he sees you with Luca. So. What is the problem? Why do you turn up on my doorstep on a Sunday morning with a face white as a bedsheet?"

Jenny continued to pick at the tablecloth. "It's more complicated," she murmured.

Gabriella threw her hands into the air in exasperation. "I cannot help if you do not tell me," she said.

"Well . . ." Jenny glanced up at her employer, at the great green eyes brimming with sympathy. "He has another mistress," she said, looking back at her hands.

"Massimo?" Gabriella exclaimed. "Oh, no, I don't think so. Not Massimo."

Jenny nodded miserably. She rubbed at her cheek with the back of one hand, destroying the last of the blusher. "She lives in Milan. Her name is Miriam, and Massimo stays with her when he goes there. I know because he had no luggage when I first met him, and he said he'd been in Milan for two weeks." Once she had begun, the words came so rapidly that they threatened to trip over one another. "And that's not all. He has a son by her! A little boy—he must be about five. He must have been born well before Teresa died. They're there now, at the apartment. I had to get out...I couldn't stay there!" Jenny stopped and took a gulp of air that turned into a little hiccup. She looked up.

Gabriella was staring at her, her scarlet mouth open and her huge eyes, outlined in black, even wider than usual. She was silent for another moment and then, to Jenny's complete dismay, she began to laugh. It was one of Gabriella's throaty whoops, loud enough to attract the curiosity of the other patrons at the little *caffè* and long enough to deprive her of the ability to talk for several unbearably long moments.

"Gabriella!" Jenny protested. "I don't see..."

Gabriella held up a hand and nodded rapidly. "I'm so sorry, dear Jennifer," she gasped. "It's just—you seem sometimes to *insist* on seeing the things wrong—you cannot simply ask the question!"

Jenny stared at the woman across from her. "I don't know what you mean," she said stiffly.

"Of course." Gabriella caught her breath, and the merriment on her face was quickly replaced by a look of warmth and sympathy. "Of course you don't. Oh, I am so sorry. Please, let me explain. And it is not funny, you are right. It was just that you seem sometimes to *work* at not understanding." Gabriella ducked her head toward Jenny and caught the younger woman's hand in her own.

"Miriam is not Massimo's mistress," she said.

Jenny blinked rapidly. "You mean you know Miriam?" she asked incredulously.

"*Si*, of course," Gabriella replied with a shrug.

"But..." Jenny ran a hand through her hair, unconsciously fluffing the waves she had so carefully brushed into it only an hour earlier. "Then who..." Bewildered, she continued to watch Gabriella's expressive face.

"Miriam is not Massimo's mistress," Gabriella repeated firmly. "And the little boy, Carlo, is not Massimo's child. He is Luca's."

Jenny shook her head wildly as the realization of what Gabriella was saying began to sink in. Miriam was Luca's lover. "No, that can't be. Not *everything* can be Luca's fault! Why is it *Massimo* who jumps when she calls, then? Why is it *Massimo* who feels an obligation...?"

Gabriella's eyes were sad. "It is because Luca feels none. And the Silvanos, they are a responsible family. Luca has had many lovers—he lives now with some film actress—but Miriam was different. She was very young and she didn't understand that Luca never intended to marry her. She *still* doesn't really understand..."

Jenny suddenly raised her hands to her cheeks. It was coming too fast, all of this. Her stomach was in turmoil, and she could hardly catch her breath. She needed to get outside, into the warm Mediterranean air—and most of all, she needed to see Massimo. The idea expanded like a balloon inside her, this need to see Massimo, until it had taken over all the available space and she could think of nothing else. She rose abruptly, pushing herself back from the table with a fierceness that threatened to tip over her chair.

"I...I have to go!" she exclaimed wildly.

Gabriella was on her feet, too, reaching out to Jenny, but Jenny was already out the door.

Chapter 10

OUTSIDE, A FINE mist had settled over *centro*. The sun, still hot and brilliant, made the damp air glitter, but it seemed to Jenny as though a thin veil had been cast over the tall, narrow gray buildings and the mazelike streets. The mist lent an undefined mystery to her surroundings. Two kittens played at fighting beside a fountain just across from the *caffè;* they reminded Jenny of the cats she and Massimo had seen on her first visit to *centro*. Except for the kittens, the street was deserted.

Jenny paused for a moment to get her bearings, took a deep breath, and set off in the direction from which she and Gabriella had come less than an hour earlier. It was all very familiar, this headlong dash through the streets and alleys of *centro*, but this time there was a difference: she was not simply proving a point. This time there was a place she wanted to be.

Despite their shroud of mist, the streets seemed neither treacherous nor hostile. There was a soft friendliness about them that almost seemed to guide Jenny around the right corners. She *remembered*—she *knew* that she and Gabriella had come down this street, had turned here . . .

Disembodied noises accompanied her: laughter rolling down the tiny spaces between the buildings from open windows three stories up; the clatter of plates and glasses as families prepared their Sunday midday meal; the echoes of Mass being said in half a dozen churches. As Jenny walked, figures appeared and disappeared in the mist ahead—even, finally, a man in a filthy sailor's jacket who fell briefly into step beside her.

She was hardly aware he was there. With fierce concentration, she studied the buildings as she hurried along, working hard to remember which ones she had passed with Gabriella. With a little smile of satisfaction, she noticed—as she had not noticed last time—the slight tilt in the streets that told her which way she was going; downward toward the sea, or upward toward the city's modern center. Carefully she kept her back to the port and wound her way out through the maze, emerging at last into the broad, busy openness of the *Piazza De Ferrari*. The sailor, unheeded, had long since disappeared.

The mist was almost nonexistent here, and a quick glance around showed Jenny a taxi rank with half a dozen vehicles waiting for customers. She clambered into the first car in line, slammed the door shut behind herself, and shouted the address of the Silvano apartment at the driver. He tipped his cap up with one finger and permitted himself a long glance in the mirror; then, evidently infected by Jenny's eagerness, he set off at a frantic pace, wheeling in and out of back streets and around parked cars, finding the fastest route up the hillside.

Jenny clutched the door handle as they careened through the streets. She wiped beads of perspiration off her forehead and her upper lip with the handkerchief she had inadvertently stuffed into her jacket pocket and patted without much result at her hair, coiled into corkscrews now from the dampness of the air.

The cab driver puffed furiously at a big, black cigar, sending periodic waves of noxious smoke into the back seat. At the crest of the hill he screeched to a halt in front of Massimo's building, then turned to face Jenny with a wide grin on his face, clearly satisfied with himself.

"*Ecco!*" he growled happily. "*È bene, sì?*"

Jenny nodded, still holding onto the door handle with one hand. "*Bene,*" she agreed faintly. She felt slightly sick to her stomach from the fumes of the cigar and the chase up the hillside, and her face must have reflected her queasiness. The driver pulled his cigar from his mouth and leaned toward her over the back of the front seat.

"*Signorina . . . ?*" he murmured, concerned.

"*Prego,*" Jenny gasped, "*uno momento, signore—non ai . . .*" Once again she found her grasp of Italian had dwindled to virtually nothing. She waved a hand vaguely toward the building. "*Non ai lire,*" she said, aware that she probably was making no sense at all. "*Aspetta, prego!*"

The driver stared at her, chewing intently on his cigar, as she pushed the taxi door open and stepped out onto the sidewalk. They were well above the damp mist here. Jenny pressed her eyes closed and inhaled a deep breath of fresh air; it was dry and crystalline, and the sky was that peculiar, overwhelmingly pure blue she had admired since the day of her arrival.

She opened her eyes a few seconds later, just in time to see the big wooden front door of the apartment building fly open. Massimo Silvano exploded through it, his face pale and drawn, his hair tumbled uncharacteristically over his forehead, and his elegant jacket unbuttoned. He was moving so quickly that he was almost past Jenny before he saw her. He stopped abruptly, his mouth slightly open.

"Jenny!" he cried. "Oh, my darling, darling Jenny! I was so frightened for you . . ."

He took a step forward, and suddenly they were in each other's arms, holding each other with all their strength. Jenny felt her legs give way, and she clung to him, letting his strong arms support her, letting him know that she needed him even for that.

"Massimo," she whispered, "I love you."

"Ah, *si, si,*" he responded softly. *"Anch'io, tesora mia.* I love you, too."

Jenny's head was buried against Massimo's broad chest, and at first she hardly heard his words. Then, slowly, she realized what he had said. She nuzzled her face into the soft white front of his shirt.

"Massimo," she murmured, "you can't imagine how much I've longed to hear you say those words..."

He stroked her hair, burying his hand in the heavy waves. Then he tilted her head back, studying her face with wide, gold-rimmed eyes, drinking in the lively fullness of her features. Jenny smiled back at him, letting her own eyes range over the planes and ridges of his face.

"I have loved you perhaps since the moment I first saw you, Jenny, standing there at the ticket counter in Milano, with your shining hair and your glowing cheeks. I was so tired of... of pale, perfect women."

Jenny stared at him. Then she closed her eyes and opened them again very slowly. "You mean I'm not perfect?" she asked.

Massimo smiled. "To me, you are perfection itself," he said firmly. He kissed the top of her head. "But I have been so worried. Gabriella just called. She told me... what you had thought... and that you had run away. She had looked for you for a few moments—oh, Jenny! I had no idea where you would go, what you would do. Gabriella, she didn't know if you understood what she had told you." Massimo wrapped his arms about Jenny again and pulled her against him.

The sound of a throat being loudly cleared interrupted their embrace. Massimo looked up. The cab driver had slid over to the passenger side of his taxi, the cigar once again planted firmly in one corner of his mouth. He was watching them with an expression of cheerful satisfaction.

"Scusi, signore," he said, sounding sincerely regretful at having to disturb them. *"Mi dispiace, ma ..."* He spread his hands in a gesture that had become familiar to Jenny in her few days in Italy—"What am I to do?" it seemed to ask. Then he rubbed the thumb and first finger of his right hand together.

Massimo laughed. "He wants his money," he said to Jenny. "Haven't you paid him?"

Jenny shook her head. "I ... I left the house without any money," she said ruefully. "I was so upset..." She ducked her head away from Massimo like a child who had done something wrong.

Massimo reached for his wallet. He paid the driver, adding a more than generous tip to the sum on the meter.

The cab driver nodded and winked. *"Grazie, signore,"* he said heartily. He glanced over at Jenny where she stood on the sidewalk, then looked back at Massimo and gave him an exaggerated thumbs-up sign of approval.

After the cab had pulled away, cigar smoke billowing out its front window, Massimo returned to Jenny's side and draped an arm over her shoulders.

"We must talk," he said firmly, moving toward the front door of the apartment building. But Jenny stopped him after a few steps.

"It's so lovely out here," she said tentatively. "Could we just ... ?"

Massimo nodded willingly. "The apartment is full of people anyway," he said. "Miriam and Carlo, and Luca."

His arm still across her shoulders, Massimo led Jenny to the low stone wall that ran behind the sidewalk and pulled her down beside him. From here they could look out over the city of Genoa, just as Jenny had on the day she had arrived. Below, in the harbor, the great ships still waited for their cargoes of freight and people; beyond, the sea shone blue under the bright sun, and small, white-capped waves danced on its surface.

"Gabriella told me what you thought," Massimo said softly. "I am so sorry—this stupid wish of mine to keep our family's shame secret—if I had only realized what you were thinking about Miriam . . ." He shook his head.

Jenny put a hand on his knee. Through the fine, light wool she could feel a tiny tremor that slowed and finally stopped beneath the touch of her fingers.

"I didn't know what to think," Jenny said. Then after a moment she corrected herself. "No, I knew just what to think. I was so sure." She shifted slightly on the wall and looked up at Massimo, wanting him to understand. "I saw her that very first day, at the Milan station. You were holding her, and she seemed so . . ." Jenny smiled wanly. "So perfect, as you say. Everything in place, so cool and calm. And there I was, frantic and exhausted and all coming to pieces. Oh, Massimo, I was so scared that I had made the wrong choice, coming to Italy—and I wanted so badly to be in control of my life!"

Massimo nodded, smiling. "So you told me," he replied dryly. "Several times."

Jenny shook her head. "How could you possibly have loved me from the start? I was behaving like such an idiot."

"You were behaving like a woman very full of adventure and wonder at life. You were wonderful."

Jenny smiled and reached one hand to his face, touching the deep creases in his cheeks. "Sometimes these look like scars," she said. "Sometimes, like that day in *centro,* or the night with Luca . . ."

Massimo took her hand in his and drew it to his mouth, kissing the palm lightly. "I am sorry if I have frightened you, my Jenny. I have frightened myself, those times. It is because I remember my wife. I wanted to protect you from being like her, but always I have realized, I have known, that you were not like her, that there was no danger like that with you."

"No," Jenny agreed. "I am not like her—not like the woman you've told me about, anyway. I . . . I will never love anyone but you."

Massimo enfolded her in his arms, burying his face in the curve of her neck and kissing the tender flesh just below her ear. Then he drew his head back again and tipped her face gently toward his with one hand.

"Let me tell you what happened. Miriam was very young when Luca decided he wanted her," he said in a soft, flat tone. "She was just seventeen. Luca was—he has always been—very attractive. And he has almost always gotten what he wanted. So he seduced Miriam."

Jenny returned Massimo's steady gaze. "You don't need to explain this . . ." she began.

He went on almost as if she had not spoken. "His other . . . conquests, I suppose one could say, had not been quite the same. They were girls of his own temperament, girls who understood what he was about. But Miriam . . . She knew only one way in which such things would end: marriage. When she became pregnant with Carlo, she assumed . . . But Luca did not marry her. He was no more interested in marrying her than in going to the moon. Miriam was made . . . a little crazy. Finally her parents, they came to *Mamma*." He paused, looking for a moment at the far off harbor, a mist covering his chestnut eyes.

"We tried to persuade Luca to marry, but there was little we could do. He has his own inheritance from my father, and *Mamma* could not bring herself to cut him off completely. Finally we made an accommodation. I would look after her and the child, and Luca would visit as often as possible. Of course," Massimo shrugged, "Luca does not visit. A child is not . . ." He shrugged again. "And Miriam is very demanding. Sometimes, like this, she just appears and I must summon Luca for her, and then she can be happy for a while."

"I'm so sorry," Jenny whispered. "I just got everything wrong. There was that picture on the piano—and then you hadn't any luggage when I first met you, yet you had been in Milan for two weeks, and I assumed . . ."

Massimo looked back at her, a hint of amusement in his eyes for the first time since he had begun speaking.

"That I had stayed with Miriam? Such an observant lady!" he said. "I had no luggage because I stay with my sister—you remember I mentioned my sister, the lawyer?—when I go to Milano. I keep a room there, and clothes. It saves trouble with packing. And the picture . . ."

He continued to look at her, but his eyes clouded again. The gold in them was still visible, but it shone softly as if through a veil. "Luca took that picture of Miriam. Every time I lose patience with her, with her constant demands and fears, I look at that picture and I see what my brother has done to her."

He shook his head again, as if attempting to clear away painful memories. But Jenny knew that this was a pain from which he would never be entirely free.

She raised a hand to his brow and brushed the thick black hair back from it. "If only you had said something earlier. Even if you had answered my questions last night."

Massimo ducked his head. *"Si,"* he agreed. "But I had no idea that you had even heard of Miriam, that you knew she existed! I should have realized, when you asked about my trips to Milano . . . but you must understand, Jenny, that Luca's behavior is painful to my family. We do not talk of it."

He looked at her again and brushed an invisible fleck off her shoulder, letting his hand rest there. His fingers traced small circles on her arm. His eyes settled on a view just beyond her, down the hillside. Jenny let her own gaze follow his, and for a moment they both sat silently, looking at the row of magnificent *palazzi* that Massimo had shown her on their tour that first day. The great palaces looked like dolls' houses from this distance, but Jenny could just pick out the one that housed the *Società*. She remembered what Massimo had said—about the forbidding walls and the hidden delights...

"And then, last night, when you asked about Miriam," Massimo finally went on, "I didn't know what to think. I didn't know what to say. I was already so confused."

Jenny gazed steadily into his eyes, feeling the warmth of his hand on her shoulder. "Why were you confused?" she asked. "Why did you pull away last night? After we had made love?"

Massimo's brow knit into a confused frown. "Because of what you said. You said that you could be happy, just as we are. I thought it must have been that your marriage ...that Simon had made you so terribly frightened of marriage that you wanted no more of it. And I..." He glanced out at the sea, glistening beneath the white-hot sun. "I cannot be happy without it."

Jenny's eyes widened in disbelief. "Oh, no—I want more than anything—" She stopped. A tiny shudder of uncertainty passed through her. Was he saying...?

Massimo smiled at her. "Want *what* more than anything? Tell me."

She sat silently, staring down at her hands where they now rested in her lap.

"May I say it, then?" he asked. Jenny could hear in his voice that same vaguely arrogant tone she had heard at their very first meeting, when he had handed her the train ticket to Genoa. It had vastly annoyed her then; now, she looked up at him, blinking her eyes expectantly.

"Will you marry me, Jennifer Armstrong?" he asked formally. "Will you become *Signora* Silvano?"

She had known what he would say, of course, but still it took her by surprise. She clutched at the stone wall, and Massimo's hand tightened on her shoulder immediately and steadied her. The chestnut eyes that were so often shielded by heavy lids or by some mysterious inner curtain were wide open now, watching her. Jenny remembered vividly how he had looked that first day in Milan: the perfectly cut suit, the graceful stride, the dazzling smile that had made her legs so suddenly weak. She studied his face now, its sharp features chiseled as if by some genius Renaissance sculptor.

Massimo laughed a deep, hearty peal of laughter. "Look at you," he cried affectionately, "with your yellow and your blue and your green and your hair the color of autumn leaves! Oh, my Jenny, I do love you!"

Jenny straightened her shoulders with a shake. "I don't see what's so funny," she said with mock indignation. Then she let a smile tip up the corners of her mouth. "I . . . I wanted to stand out next to Miriam."

Massimo rocked with laughter. "From now on, we must tell each other everything. Every doubt, every worry. We must never let anything like this happen again."

Jenny nodded. "Deal," she said, holding out her hand to shake his.

Massimo looked at her. "Deal?" he asked.

"That means we promise," she said. "Just like in business."

He nodded and took her hand, shaking it firmly. "Ah," he said. "It's a deal."

"Oh, and about marrying you," Jenny went on. Massimo looked at her expectantly. "The answer is yes."

Epilogue

JENNY HAD LEARNED that the city of Genoa was hot and still in late summer, and that anyone who could moved farther east, away from the port where the indentation of the coast held the hot, wet summer air in place day after day.

Having returned from their wedding voyage to Venice, Jenny and Massimo lolled on the lawn of the senior *Signora* Silvano's *villa* in Rapallo, enjoying the sun and watching Nino and Angela play happily by the pool. Out to sea, a swift-running sailboat glided across the smooth blue surface of the Mediterranean, its snowy sails billowing in the soft breeze.

Jenny's arm tightened around Massimo's waist, and she slid her hand beneath his shirt, feeling the hard, strong muscles of his back. Her bare thigh touched his; the myriad tiny black hairs tickled her leg.

"I'd like to learn to sail," she said lazily, watching the progress of the boat.

"That could certainly be arranged," Massimo replied, rolling over on his side to look at her. He touched her hair with his hand, and she felt once again the tiny shock of electricity that always accompanied his touch. "I could teach you myself."

Jenny propped her head on one hand and looked at her husband. "That would be perfect," she said, grinning. "You see, I had a dream once, on the train from Milan to Genoa . . ."

All of the above titles are $1.75 per copy except where noted